PENGUIN BOOKS

KATIE GOES TO KL

Su-May Tan was born and raised in Malaysia but is currently living on Wurundjeri land in Melbourne. Her debut short story collection *Lake Malibu and other stories* was shortlisted for the Queensland Literary Awards 2022. Having moved to Melbourne in 2012, she often writes on themes of migration and cultural connection. Website: sumaytan.com.

ADVANCE PRAISE FOR *KATIE GOES TO KL*

'Su-May Tan's writing is lush and original, her characters compelling, her voice mesmerizing. She captures the longings of youth and the ache of displacement with beauty and vivacity. A stunning debut.'

—Kathryn Heyman, novelist

'I love Su-May Tan's writing. Her Malaysia and Australia are complex, vivid places, where ambition, hunger, family and friendship intertwine in funny, tender ways. Her quietly distinct voice is a gift to Australian storytelling.'

—James Button, author and ex-journalist, *The Age*

Katie Goes to KL

Su-May Tan

PENGUIN BOOKS

An imprint of Penguin Random House

PENGUIN BOOKS

USA | Canada | UK | Ireland | Australia
New Zealand | India | South Africa | China | Southeast Asia

Penguin Books is part of the Penguin Random House group of companies
whose addresses can be found at global.penguinrandomhouse.com

Published by Penguin Random House SEA Pte Ltd
9, Changi South Street 3, Level 08-01,
Singapore 486361

First published in Penguin Books by Penguin Random House SEA 2023
Copyright © Su-May Tan 2023

ISBN 9789815127812

Typeset in Garamond by MAP Systems, Bengaluru, India

www.penguin.sg

Disclaimer

This is a work of fiction. This story takes place in a reimagined Malaysia. All characters, places and occurrences are fictionalized and do not represent actual happenings in the country and any resemblance to actual persons, living or dead, places or occurrences is purely coincidental. Nothing in this book is intended to cause offence or to hurt the sentiments of any individual, community, section of people, group or religion. Any liability arising from any action undertaken by any person by relying upon any part of this book is strictly disclaimed.

Part I

Melbourne

Chapter 1

The Banana Tree and the Cat

My mother died when I was seven. There are signs of her around, if you care to look. Like the *batik* prints on the wall or the beaded purse in the sideboard drawer. If you go outside, you can see a banana tree standing in the middle of the garden, probably the only banana tree in Narre Warren.

'Why don't we get rid of it?' I told Pa. He said, 'No, just give it time. It will do better next year.' And so, we live in this house with a white picket fence and a banana tree that looks like it's going to die.

* * *

For someone who has lived in Australia for ten years, Pa spends an awful lot of time reading Malaysian news. Whenever he does, he gets really cross. There's always some politician he's grumbling about or some news report that makes him annoyed. Diana often says, 'You've left the country, why don't you just let it go?' She says this in her psychologist voice—a soft, quiet voice that could be your own. It's the same voice she uses when she sees me heading off to the park. 'Are you going by yourself? Will you get back before dark?'

Dessi, my best friend, comes over a lot. We met a few years ago at the grotto of St Mary of the Angels while the grown-ups were in church. This girl wore long stripey stocks way before long stripey socks came into fashion. 'Where's your mum?' she asked. That's when I found out her mum was divorced. We became friends, sisters of the grotto, allowed to escape church because the Sunday School teacher thought we would benefit more from some 'quiet, meditative time' outside rather than listening to Father Andrew talk about the gospel of the day.

One Friday after school, Dessi followed me down the driveway and said, 'Oh my god! look.'

'What?'

She pointed at the banana tree. There on a stalk, hung three combs of mini green fingers. After all these years, it had finally bloomed! I imagined my mother planting a mini version of this plant in the ground all those years ago. Ten years of sitting alongside blue gums and bottlebrushes looking like an out-of-place guest, today it finally decided to show its true colours. I bent down closer to examine the large pink bud at the end—I didn't even know it grew that way.

I should have suspected something then but Dessi and I continued our evening in the usual manner. We trudged into the pantry, looking for snacks. I found some Big M in the fridge, Dessi discovered a box of Cruskits. 'No pandan cake today?' she asked, examining the shelves.

'No, my dad didn't make any.'

'Your dad makes the best food!' gushed Dessi. 'When is he going to make that pork jerky again? Is it bak kwa?'

'Yeah, bak kwa,' I mumbled flatly, though Dessi must be the only Greek person in the world who knew what bak kwa was.

We poured out the last of the Big M and took large frothy sips. I could see the crack of light underneath Pa's study in the room opposite mine. When he got back from the biscuit factory, he locked himself in there for hours. I heard the sound of a thud or something heavy being moved. 'What does he do in there?' asked Dessi.

I shrugged. 'He's just on the computer a lot.'

'Online dating?' Dessi smirked. 'Or,' she gasped. 'Maybe he's a spy. Does he go out at odd hours? Seen any trace of ammunition?'

I gave her a dry look and slurped up the rest of my milk. It tickled my throat and I began coughing. Was it a virus? Had I caught something from the pool? It had taken me months to convince myself that the pool water was clean though I always rinsed off fully as soon as I got out. 'Do you think I have pneumonia?' I asked.

'No.'

'Why not?'

'You've had this cough since we first met.' That was true. But that didn't mean it wasn't pneumonia. I reached for a Vitamin C supplement and popped it into my mouth. Thank God for Vitamin C. As we marched up the stairs, I sucked on the pellet, revelling in the knowledge of an army building up in my body, ready to protect me from whatever nasties there were in the world.

* * *

Dessi plopped onto the bed and took out the manga she had been reading. I went straight to my desk and opened up my maths textbook. Let's see, ten questions today—that wouldn't take too long. Once I finished that, I could get started on the science project. I loved this thrill of lining things up in my head. I gave myself exactly forty minutes for maths so I would be finished by 5 p.m., leaving me with just enough time to jump onto science.

As I opened my pencil case, I found my gaze wandering towards my dresser. The items there were arranged in perfect order: toner, moisturizer, hairbrush. Hang on—what was my thermometer doing out there? I went over and put it back into my toilet case. Then I went back to the desk and checked my stationery: two red pens, one blue—where was the other blue one? I checked the floor and found it next to the lamp cable.

Dessi remained sprawled on the bed, one finger dawdling on the page in front of her. A few minutes later, she said, 'What's happening with your dad and Diana?'

'What?'

Dessi gestured at the window. Diana and Pa were standing outside underneath the banana tree. 'What do you mean?' I asked.

'Are they like going out?'

'Of course not.'

Diana laughed and picked something off Pa's shoulder.

'Really?' Dessi narrowed her eyes.

It was at times like these that I wondered even more about her. This pang, the shape of my fist, the shape of this person standing next to my father. I opened my jewellery box without thinking and picked up the silver comb inside. It wasn't a 'comb' comb, more like a clip you were supposed to fix onto your hair.

She'd had long black hair—not like Diana's salon curls or Dessi's wavy locks—but thick Asian hair like the lady in the YouTube video I'd Googled to see how one used a hair comb. What did she sound like? What did she look like? I couldn't picture it. Every time I tried to conjure it up, I saw the Chinese lady in the video smiling at the camera, a little frozen, slipping the metal comb into a twisted knot of hair.

'You at it again?' said Dessi.

'What?' I quickly put the comb away and snapped my jewellery box shut.

'You're not the only one who's lost a parent, you know.'

I traced the corner of my textbook. 'Don't you ever wonder about your dad?'

'No.' Dessi sniffed and turned the page.

I bit the tip of my pen and observed Dessi's calm cool shape on my bed, the purple streak in her hair reflecting the sun. 'What does your mum say about him?' I asked.

'Nothing. I haven't seen him since he left. Oh, I lie. I saw him once at Woolies, with some skinny blonde girl,' she said with a snicker.

'You mean he still lives here in Narre Warren?'

'Yeah.' Dessi flicked her hair and turned the page.

'And you don't see him?'

'Nope,' she replied, without even looking up.

Dessi continued to read. I returned to my homework but a heaviness had descended upon the room. It stayed there after Dessi left, after I'd brushed my teeth and as I was combing the knots out of my hair I was plagued by this feeling that something was about to happen. And then I saw it.

The cat stood on the sill outside my window. I hadn't seen it since I was eight. I had tried to tell Pa then. 'Look, Pa,' I said. 'A cat.'

'You mean a possum?'

'No, a cat,' I said, pointing my stubby finger at it.

The cat had continued to come day after day, then every other week, then one day it stopped and I forgot it had ever come, until now. Why had it come back? Was it the same one? Orange stripes, grey eyes. It blinked at me—once, twice, then disappeared into the darkness.

Chapter 2

School

Pa rarely took me to school but of all the days he could've picked, he decided to do it on the day of the audition. 'You can just drop me here,' I said, gesturing towards the bus stop.

'No, I can turn in,' he insisted.

'No, really, that way you won't have to make a U-turn.'

'It's okay, I don't have to go into work as early today.'

I clutched the handle of my bag, feeling the hard leather against my palm as Pa drove past the bus stop and turned onto Watsons Road, past the new townhouses, past the vet with the giant giraffe and towards the gates of Valewood High. We joined a queue of cars crawling along a street lined with trees I knew by heart: a stringybark, a bottlebrush, a blue gum with a silvery white trunk.

'I told you there would be a jam,' I muttered.

'It's okay, I have time today. You've got guitar today?'

'Yeah.'

He glanced at the boot where my guitar case sat. 'What song are you learning now?'

I said nothing about the audition. 'Just the same one.' I shifted in my seat and peered at his profile. 'Why are you wearing that?'

'Wearing what?'

'That jacket.'

'I always wear this jacket.'

'It looks so . . . Chinese.'

'What do you mean?'

I pressed my mouth shut and peered out the window. We crept closer to the front gate where the Year 11 and 12 students were hanging out. It was a new recreational area for senior students—outdoor study areas not unlike the ones you'd see on university campuses. The only problem was, everyone tended to hang around there and you had to march down this walkway to get to the main building.

One car stopped in front of us and then another. Familiar faces began to step out: Jessica Coleman, Riley Dwyer, Mac Bailey. Each swinging their backpacks into the air and letting the sun embrace them, highlighting the gold in their hair, the paleness of their skin. When my turn came, I quickly did the same. I hurled my backpack over my shoulder and said a quick goodbye to Pa.

'Bye,' he called out. I had already slammed the door shut. I grabbed my guitar case from the boot and hurried towards the classrooms, ignoring the stares and whispers on either side: 'Oh, there she is.' 'Look it's "Mr Miyagi's" daughter'.

I imagined them commenting on the way I walked, the way I moved. I was reminded of this comic I'd read when I was younger, wherein a cat asked a dog how he walked. Did he go two front feet first or left front then right front, and when the dog thought about it, he could never walk again.

I focused on putting one foot in front of the other, stepping within the lines of the concrete slabs. If I stepped on any of the grooves, I would be in trouble. If I managed to make it through cleanly, I would be fine. The familiar doors of the library were just ahead. They beckoned me towards the sanctuary of its shelves and aisles, where I could hide and wait until the bell rang.

* * *

The audition was right after lunch. I'd been thinking about it all day, all through science class and English, feeling this knot growing in my stomach—and now it was here. The curtains blew towards me; stiff, stale velvet, holding the nerves of performers in the roughness of its fabric. Before me lay a sea of muted shadows. I heard the creak of a seat and everything turned black. A laser light shone down on me abruptly. I could feel its rays almost severing my arms.

Three people sat in the first row. Others lurked in the distance but it was only the three people in front that mattered. I took a deep breath and began. The guitar felt heavy under my arm as I plunged into the notes I had played a thousand times before. And yet, I stumbled through the curves and bends, barely managing to scrape through a little dip I had forgotten was there. Before I knew it, I arrived at the thrill section and my fingers froze. 'Come on,' I thought, willing them to move. Each time I started, I fell. I skipped to the next line and it happened again. Maybe they didn't notice, maybe it wasn't that bad. I kept going and moved on to the Legato bit, when one of the judges—a lady in green—told me to stop.

Please, let me try again.

'Thank you,' she said with a curt nod. And that was the end. The satin of her blouse shimmered. Her pen clicked shut.

When I stepped out into the sunlight, I was blinded by the brightness. Then it cleared and I saw groups of people loitering around. Jessica Coleman's mum gave her a hug—she looked like an older version of Jessica with her shiny blonde hair. Anya's mum beamed and showered her daughter with a bunch of flowers.

'Hey Katie, how did it go?' Jessica Coleman asked, all white teeth and sunshine.

'Um . . .'

'You didn't get through? That's okay! I heard Cindy Lewis is really difficult to work with, so—'

As Jessica Coleman continued to talk, her words washed over me like paint, covering me in a crappy pink shade that grew brighter and hotter with each passing second. My cheeks grew warm, my throat seized up. The more she spoke, the tighter my chest became. I clutched my guitar case to beat the urge to run. Were people staring? Could they see my flushed face?

'Katie, there you are.' Dessi's voice cut through the noise like a train. 'Come on.' She linked her arm with mine and steered me towards the gate. 'Bitch,' she muttered, as we stepped out onto the footpath.

'What do you mean?'

'She knew you didn't get through. I saw her watching from the stands.'

Dessi went on talking all the way to the bus stop. I hated carrying that big guitar case with me. I wished it was smaller. I wished I could just chuck it away. I focused on my white Fila shoes, placing one foot in front of the other. I tried to breathe more slowly. The tightness in my chest did not subside until I saw the familiar Bulla poster at the bus stop. The same poster that was there in the morning. For some reason, that image of milk being poured into an ice-cream tub made me feel less stressed.

The 206 came and left. It would be another fifteen minutes before the Number 19 arrived. I spotted an unusual black stain on the floor, presumably from a lolly or spilt Coke, and inched my guitar case away from it. Across the road, Jessica Coleman emerged, surrounded by a gaggle of girls. Her mother was nowhere to be seen. The group of girls crossed the road, their too-short skirts revealing legs tanned from weekends at Mentone Beach or wherever people like them hung out. Dessi opened up a book and began to read, as oblivious to Jessica and her crew as they were to us. They gathered at the far end of the bus stop talking about going to Chaddy while taking peeks at each other's phones. We were as insignificant as the dustbin overflowing with

Subway sandwich wrappers. Jessica laughed and suddenly it all
went silent.

You could feel the change in the air. That sudden zap of
electricity. A truck rolled by and the navy blazers of the St Patrick's
boys appeared at the end of the street. Navy blazers with that
streak of white that marked them as the boys from St Patrick's
and not the public school down the road. Among them was John
Ichuda, with his milky white skin and a smile that lit up the streets
of Narre Warren. When he went to work at Woolies, people would
line up in his aisle just to bask in the glow of his presence. When
he turned up at the country club, they would stop to chat and
admire the white polo shirt skimming over his shoulders. They
never hesitated to spare a moment for this charming young man,
who was captain of the tennis team and the top-voted 'Person
I Would Most Like to Marry' in the secret diaries of girls from
Valewood High.

Jessica radiated an even brighter glow, flicking away locks that
had landed her a shampoo commercial (though Dessi thinks that
was a self-fabricated rumour). The St Patrick's boys pretended not
to stare.

'Oh,' I said.

'What?' said Dessi, eyes fixed on her book.

'I got a message.'

'From whom?'

I glanced up. He was gazing casually into the distance. Jessica
Coleman remained at the other side of the bus stop—not on her
phone. She was chatting still with her friends, showing them her
latest manicure.

John Ichuda and I exchanged a few more texts. It was like
the day when we spoke at the scholarship tuition and all those
other times while waiting for our parents to come pick us up. We
always seemed to be the last two to get picked up, or at least it
felt that way. I don't even remember what we spoke about. I just

remember how close he stood next to me outside the Salvation Army shop as the evening turned dark.

I looked up and saw him smile at his phone. We texted about frivolous things like the weather and school—then his question arrived and I almost dropped my phone.

John Ichuda : Do you want to go to the Spring Dance with me?

I showed Dessi the screen. 'What do I say?'

Dessi rolled her eyes and turned back to her book. 'Well, you've only been in love with him for like two years.' And so I gripped my phone and replied just as a spray of wattle floated past. The yellow flowers fell around us in slow-motion as the Number 19 bus broke through the afternoon: a knight, a chariot slicing the sun and splintering it into a zillion rays.

Chapter 3

The Phone Call

It was all I could think about that night as I checked my temperature through my ear. John Ichuda and me. At the Spring Dance. I popped the thermometer back into my toilet case and pictured his hazel eyes looking down at me. I tried to decipher which part of his face was Japanese and which was Swedish. They swirled together in a mix of mahogany hair and pale skin. Did he really want to go with me?

My mirror revealed a plain-faced girl with bright brown eyes—not small but small enough to be called cute. I cleansed my face with toner, then applied a perfectly round drop of moisturizer, examining my complexion from different angles. Was it me or was my skin a bit more radiant tonight?

I suppose some people might consider me . . . sweet? 'Beautiful' seemed too strong. Adjectives like 'hot' and 'beautiful' were reserved for girls like Jessica Coleman with their big, bold looks. I was smallish; slight, if you like. Not skinny per se, but I had slim ankles and slim. In actual fact, I wore size 10 clothing, probably the same as Jessica Coleman, but the same dress would look mighty different on Jessica and on me, especially around the bust area.

My best feature? I narrowed my eyes at the mirror and the girl staring back at me did too. Everything about me seemed mediocre. Medium, mediocre Katie. Average eyes, average height, averagely pretty. Dessi said I had nice hair—shiny black hair that was neither too thin or thick. I suppose black stands out when you're in a world of blondes and browns.

Had her hair been like that too? My thoughts drifted to her, as they sometimes did. She remained a shadow in the dark. Even when I tried to squeeze out the memories or recall old photos, I came up with nothing. Pa only had that one picture of her— how could that be possible? From that photo, I surmised she was slight too, though it was hard to tell in the wedding dress.

Speaking of love—John Ichuda. I carefully placed my moisturizer back on the table and tried to figure out what to wear. The perfect outfit came to me—that blue dress from Sports Girl! It had a plain cotton bodice but the skirt was made of a gossamer blue material. There was something about gossamer I liked—that mysterious quality of something that was there or not quite there. A holder of secrets; the flight of a dragonfly; something a little like magic.

Perhaps she had worn it too, at an event I couldn't remember. Dessi had asked me once, what was my earliest memory of her. She was reading a book about memory and the human brain at the time. (Dessi tends to go all-out when a topic strikes her fancy.) The earliest memory I have is of blowing out candles on my birthday. I think I may have been two years old. Dessi says it's a lie. She says people can't really remember anything before the age of three because of childhood amnesia. Maybe she is right. Because I can't really remember anything about her. She is just this shadowy shape that appears and disappears. A hand holding mine; a skirt fluttering at her knees. When I look up, I can only see the sun shining in my eyes.

I went to sleep with a flutter in my chest, the blankets pulled right up to my chin, and drifted into a restful slumber. The ringing must have happened at about 3 a.m. when I was in the deepest sleep. The eucalyptus tree in our yard, the Blue Gum, tapped on my window and then the cat appeared. 'Pick up,' he said.

'What?'

'Pick up.' Its mouth was closed and yet I knew the voice was coming from him. The ringing sound continued, getting louder, like a phone in a distant universe. For some reason, I could not move. It was like an invisible weight was sitting on me. 'Pa,' I said, 'the phone is ringing.' This time, I could not move my mouth. 'Pa!' I called in my head, 'The phone!' The yellow eyes continued to burn. The cat began to change. It turned into a possum, then into a fox, then into a tawny frogmouth, like the one I saw at the park last week.

It was at this point that I woke up, or at least I think I did. The shadows in my room snatched me back into the present. I saw the shape of my chair, a sliver of light between the blinds. A moment later, I fell back asleep and drifted into a misty cavern, where there were no cats or owls or dreams.

* * *

The next morning, I opened my bedroom door to welcome a perfectly sunny Saturday. Everything was dripping with light as if it had rained inside—the glass on the window, the gleaming banister. I padded down the stairs and when I reached the bottom, I heard the creak of a chair. Diana's low voice. Pa's rumbling reply. Then silence. I was about to take another step when Diana's voice cut through the air. 'Will she be there?'

Pa's response was muffled by the sound of boiling water. I froze in the shadow of the doorway, straining to make out the rest of his words. I heard only a clock ticking, the clink of a spoon. When I stepped into the light, Pa froze ever so slightly, his fist clenched in his lap. Diana whipped her head around and cleared her throat.

'Hi Katie,' she said, her voice bright and cheery.

'Hi.'

'Did you have a good sleep?' Diana's eyes twinkled like a young girl's. If she wore a T-shirt or a uniform, you would think she was sixteen, but most of the time, she was dressed in her office clothes—a silky blouse tucked into a fitted skirt. 'You guys are up early,' I mumbled. Pa didn't move. He remained seated at the table, eyes glazed. Diana gave him a quick glance before replying. 'Your dad had an early morning call.'

'I thought I heard the phone,' I commented.

Pa sat quietly, a Kathmandu jacket thrown over his pyjamas. His clothes always seemed a little oversized but that day, they looked especially voluminous. 'What's wrong?' I asked. 'Is Pa okay?'

'Yeah,' replied Diana, taking out two mugs from a cupboard. Pa scratched his head. He radiated with a glow as if he had been working in the sun all day. But he had always been like this—tanned and glowing as if he'd brought the tropics with him from Malaysia.

'So, who called?' I said.

Pa peered at me with bleary, red eyes. 'Ah Ma passed away last night,' he said in a hoarse voice. He continued to speak as the camellias bloomed outside; as Diana poured hot water into the cups. He must have told me how she died, who was there and what to do, but my mind was too busy thinking about John Ichuda and the date we would never have.

'When do we have to go?' I asked. The scenes in my head continued to rush past as a dark pit formed in my stomach.

'Tomorrow,' Pa replied in a firm voice.

'For how long?'

'Just a couple of weeks.'

I flinched. Every second seemed like a second too long, slug after slug at my dreams which were already dangling by threads. 'What about school?' I stammered.

'You have term break in a couple of weeks, right?' said Pa. 'You'll only miss what, two weeks?'

It wasn't about the length of time. It wasn't about school. It was about that Saturday that would change my life, the nineteenth of September when John Ichuda and I were going to have the most beautiful night of our lives; the start of our wondrous relationship.

'Why do I need to go?' I blurted. 'I don't even know her.'

Pa whipped his head up and looked at me with stern eyes. 'Because we're family.'

Family? When did he ever care about family? He'd hardly ever gone back and never even called Ah Ma.

Diana slid a mug in front of Pa. He did not touch it. 'The taxi will be here at six-thirty in the morning,' Pa said, calmly folding his arms. Hearing his tone, I knew there was no way out of this one. The Spring Dance was gone. My dress of gossamer blue gave a final twinkle before dissipating into nothing. Three weeks. Three weeks would pass by pretty quickly, wouldn't they? We could message. We could chat.

'Are you going?' I asked Diana.

'Umm . . .' She glanced at Pa. His eyes remained locked on the table. Diana gripped her mug and said, 'No, I don't think I will.'

'Why not?' I said. 'We can all go together.'

Diana flicked back her curls. 'I can't, sweetie,' she replied. 'I've got to work.' She finished the last of her tea and got up. Her cup made a cold clinking sound on the table. I watched her wash her hands and flick them dry. After she left, the smell of her dewberry shampoo lingered in the room.

Chapter 4

On the Plane

The last time I was in Malaysia, I was six years old. My memories of the place were intertwined with programmes I'd seen on TV such that I no longer knew which memories were from the TV shows and which were real. Twenty thousand feet below, I pictured tropical forests and bustling markets like I'd seen on *Street Food Asia*. Malaysia, to me, was this small protrusion on a map which I had to talk about at Show and Tell in Prep. It was the food we went to eat at restaurants alongside other people who sounded like Pa.

Around me, tables snapped up and passengers shrugged off the mustiness of sleep. I, too, wriggled out of the hunched position I had been in for the last eight hours. Pa sat beside me and shook out a page of the *Financial Times*. How could he be so calm? Was he actually looking forward to returning? I had no idea what to expect. This was not like going to the Gold Coast or a resort in Bali. We would be staying in someone's house. I would be stuck with Pa for three weeks with us having nothing to say to each other. If Diana was coming, at least we could have hung out.

A lady pulled out her Country Road sweater from underneath her and I was reminded of how much I hated air travel. The smell of stale perfume and unbrushed teeth. The static of human bodies. I pushed my table back up with one finger. How many people had sat on these seats before me, touched these very tables with hands that had been to so many places. I took out a wet wipe and began scrubbing my fingers.

The aeroplane made a slow sharp turn. Houses dotted the land like a monopoly board and a thick brown river snaked through it. Nothing about the land below looked familiar. I felt myself being taken further and further away from my life and the world I knew—just as it had begun to get better. As we descended the mass of trees below grew bigger. I thought of the picture of my cousin, Roy and I, framed and kept on the piano back home. We must have been about four or five—our cheeks chubby, our grins toothy—as we stood on a bridge, smiling at the camera. Was the Japanese Garden somewhere down there? What would Roy look like now? If I was sixteen, he must be seventeen.

My heart thrummed with excitement. I imagined us hugging and hanging out the way only family could, talking and laughing about everything and nothing in particular. Would he remember feeding the terrapins in the pond? Would he remember playing hide-and-seek?

My ears clogged up. The plane sank lower. Things that had merely been shapes before, took on more detail. A dot turned into a logging truck. A brown patch turned into a lake. Somewhere on the highway, a red sedan inched along like a moving target. As the clouds broke past my window, more memories sped in: Chinese New Year, Ah Ma's house, getting *angpows* from aunties and uncles. A gentle peace bubbled inside me as I descended into Kuala Lumpur—into KL—the land of my birth.

Part II

Malaysia

Chapter 5

The Airport

Hot air hit me like a truck. Trolleys rolled left and right. Signs said 'exit' in three different languages. I wove through the masses of people, keeping my eye on the orange ribbon of Pa's Delsey suitcase. We stopped every few steps to let people pass. First, it was an elderly couple, then a swarm of school kids. Pa continued weaving in and out, following an invisible path only he could see. For a moment, I lost him, then I saw the orange ribbon bobbing out the automatic doors.

'Taxi, taxi,' a man said to Pa. He was dressed in a blue polo T-shirt and had a shifty way of looking around. 'Taxi, taxi,' he said again, as if offering us drugs. Pa waved him off and continued to trundle down the pavement.

We stopped at Bay 8. Pa checked his phone as my gaze followed the crack of a broken pillar up to the ceiling. The warm air wrapped around me like a blanket I could not fling off. I could smell every single scent there was—tarmac, cigarettes, fried noodles from a café—swirling together like a thick, black soup.

Everything began to happen at the same time. A red car double-parked in front of a white one. A boy started bawling. A man walked by, yelling into his mobile phone. Out of this chaos, a lady appeared. People seemed to part as she floated towards us, a figure you could not ignore in shimmery black palazzo pants and a flowy blouse the colour of mango.

This was Tua Ee. For the longest time, I thought that was her Chinese name. It meant 'Eldest Aunty' and that's who she was to me. When she reached us, she whipped off a pair of sunglasses twinkling with diamonds. 'Ah Choon,' she said, calling Pa by his Chinese name. They hugged and I tried not to stare at Tua Ee's eyebrows, two painted arches on her cakey white face.

'This Katie?' Tua Ee gushed. 'Wah, so big already.'

'Hello Tua Ee, how are you?' I leaned forward to give her a hug and a whiff of flowers puffed towards me.

She let out a weak laugh. 'How was your flight?'

'Good—' I began.

'What's that?' She pointed beside me.

'My guitar,' I clutched the handle with two hands.

'Wah, so clever, I don't think anyone in the family can play anything.' Tua Ee's eyes shone, studying the curve of the case.

I kept my eyes fixed on her. 'My mum played the piano,' I said.

Tua Ee froze. Her tangerine lips parted, setting off the auburn in her eyebrows.

Pa cleared his throat and frowned. 'She means Sue,' he added in a hushed voice.

'Oh.' A pair of stewardesses sashayed by, their sandals making clackety noises on the pavement. Tua Ee glanced at the sky. 'Looks like it's going to rain. We better get going.' She thrust out a shiny gold heel and hurried towards the cars.

Chapter 6

The Drive Back

Tua Ee drove the same way she walked through the airport. Cars seemed to move out of her way as if she were driving a bulldozer and not a little Honda Civic. As she broke out of the exit, she asked Pa, 'How's work?'

'Okay.'

'Still at the factory?'

'Yes.'

Tua Ee didn't say anything but I noticed how she gripped the steering wheel and clenched her jaw. Pa used to be a journalist, now he worked at this biscuit factory in Hallam. If he felt uncomfortable, he didn't show it. He continued gazing out the window. 'The jungle is all gone,' he mused.

'Yes, all palm oil now,' said Tua Ee.

We passed row after row of chunky stout palms, each one identical to the next. Was this the greenery I'd seen from the plane? I'd imagined a sea of rainforest like in those Tourism Malaysia ads. 'Katie,' Tua Ee caught my eye through the rear view mirror. 'You remember Roy and Maggie?'

'Yes.'

'They can't wait to see you.'

I smiled back, a small ball beginning to fizz in my chest.

Tua Ee stopped the car beside a booth. She handed some notes to the lady inside and the barrier in front of us magically lifted. The highway merged into a series of lanes, the road flanked by petrol stations, shops and office blocks. As we took the flyover on the right, Pa said, 'What happened to Jalan Templer?'

'Didn't you hear? They changed it to Jalan Kamaruddin.'

'Not another one.'

'They've changed so many road names already. Campbell Street, Jalan Alor, Green Street . . .'

'Yeah.' Pa squinted out the window again. Even from that angle, I could see a furrow on his brow. I tried to figure out what he was staring at. I saw a mosque, a bus stop, a playground with a rusty slide. When we reached a traffic light, I saw a woman standing on the kerb waiting to cross. She was draped in black from head to toe—black face covering, black robe, long black skirt—her eyes peering through a small dark slit. I couldn't stop staring at this apparition, black as night in the afternoon sun, her headscarf billowing around her as if she belonged in the middle of the Sahara and not here, facing an MNG billboard with Justin Bieber blasting out of Tua Ee's radio singing: 'I won't give up, nah-nah-nah. Let me love you, let me love you'.

* * *

When we reached a housing estate, Tua Ee slowed down. We passed house after house, each with a sharp metal fence that seemed serious about keeping people out. Finally, she stopped in front of a big black gate. I peered through the bars and saw a concrete driveway leading up to a double-storey house, its front wall splashed with mustard.

In the garden, a palm tree rose high but it was the tree next to it that caught my attention. It looked like it was sprouting pink plastic bags. Pa said they were mangoes. The plastic bags around them were meant to protect them from being eaten by the birds. Tua Ee stepped out of the car and yelled, 'We're back!'

At first, there was nothing, the house just blinked in the sun. Then the door grille creaked open. A man stepped out in a smart button-down shirt but as he approached, I noticed a pair of thongs on his feet. *Flip-flop flip-flop*, he padded towards us, clearing his throat as he fiddled with the gate. 'Tua Teow,' whispered Pa to me.

'Hello Tua Teow,' I said to my Eldest Uncle. 'How are you?'

He cleared his throat again. 'Fine, thank you.'

Tua Ee continued to bark orders at various people. She asked a girl to help with the suitcases. She asked Tua Teow to hold the front door open. Then she asked Roy to grab the pomelos from the boot. *Roy!* I watched him stride to the back of the car, big manly Roy in a baggy T-shirt with thick black and white stripes. Roy, who did not look like the little boy in the photo at all, with his muscled arms and long gait. Pa made his way to the front door and slipped off his shoes. I did the same.

We entered a living room furnished with rattan furniture and marble tiles that were cool under my feet. I followed Pa down a corridor and we emerged into a kitchen. There was a large table there and a few people were already seated around it. A girl with short curly hair came to greet us. *Could this be Maggie?* I tried to recall what she looked like but I could only picture a vague being smaller than Roy.

The girl in front of me had tanned, lean limbs. She wore a large baggy T-shirt with the words 'Ambank Ultra Run' on it, beneath a graphical drawing of some buildings. 'Did you do a marathon?' I pointed to her T-shirt. She smiled at me shyly.

'What do you want to drink?' boomed Tua Ee. 'Orange juice, Coca-Cola, chrysanthemum tea?'

'Tea would be nice,' I replied, imagining a nice warm cuppa.

The girl ran off and came back carrying a small yellow carton. 'Thank you,' I said, examining the box, which said 'Yeo's

Chrysanthemum Tea'. 'I've never seen tea like this before.' The girl giggled and Tua Ee told me this was Siti, her helper from Indonesia. I glanced at the girl, then back down again, a hot flush rising in my cheeks.

Pa and I joined the others around the kitchen table. Most of them seemed to know me. A man with silver-rimmed glasses beamed. 'Wah, Katie, so big already. Last time I saw you, you were this high.' He gestured to a point near his waist.

'She looks so much like you,' exclaimed the lady next to Pa. 'She's got your nose.'

'Her eyes are different, though,' the man mused, studying my face. The table turned silent. Tua Teow froze, a prawn gripped between his chopsticks, shiny with oil.

'Aiya, must be the *ang moh* weather there,' snapped Tua Ee. 'See her cheeks, all rosy also.'

The conversation turned to politics. They talked about scandals and the coming elections, and this guy, Tun Said, who was the leader of some Islamic group.

'Can you believe they voted him as the Wira chief?'

'Crazy fella. Did you hear how he wanted to burn down a church?'

Pa started telling them about a speech this guy made. I began to zone out. I didn't understand the dynamics of the situation, plus it was hard to understand their accents. I turned my attention to the food on the table: fried noodles in black sauce and okra stuffed with fish paste. I chose an okra and Tua Ee said, 'Oh, you know how to eat lady's fingers'. She said I was 'very clever' to eat it, and I wondered what kind of intelligence one needed to consume a vegetable.

Chapter 7

Cousins

Roy had not said a word to me all morning, except for the time he had helped carry our bags into the house. He was now sitting with some friends at the dining table. The three of them, all boys, were playing cards.

'Can I play?' I said, sliding into one of the chairs.

Roy narrowed his eyes at me. 'You know how to play?'

'Is it poker?'

'No, *Chor Tai Tee.*'

'Oh,' I said. 'Maybe I'll just watch.'

Roy shuffled the cards. He dealt out the deck, giving thirteen cards to each person and opening the last one face up. The boys picked and threw cards, moving around in a circle until it was Roy's turn again.

There was not much of the boy in the photo left in him, except maybe the eyes. He still had small shiny eyes like some kind of imp. They played two rounds of the game and throughout that time, Roy did not say a word to me. He did not even glance my way. As he started shuffling the next round, I got up and walked over to the sofas.

Tua Ee had introduced me to Maggie earlier and I spotted her sitting in front of the TV with a friend. Poised on the seat in her short slick bob, she looked nothing like Siti. Her skin was fair, her lips painted a bright cherry red. 'I love your hair,' she said as I sat down beside her. 'Do you curl it?'

'No.' I stifled a laugh.

'So lucky,' she gushed. 'I wish I had thicker hair.'

Maggie turned to her friend and continued to chat away. I watched them chirping in various tones, throwing their heads back to laugh as their nails gleamed in the light of the room. They could have been birds at a park.

Maggie, as if suddenly sensing my gaze, turned back to me. 'Do you speak Mandarin?' she asked.

'No, not really,' I mumbled, feeling a prickle at my neck.

'Hokkien?'

'A little bit.'

'You're Hokkien, right?' Maggie narrowed her silver-dusted eyes at me.

'Well, my father is . . .' I said, fidgeting with my fingers.

'So you only speak English?' Maggie continued to stare at me with wide, innocent eyes.

'Yes,' I stammered, feeling my cheeks grow warm.

Applause broke out on the TV screen and I saw a man stride up onto the stage. I said he looked a bit like George Liao from *The Voice*.

'Who?'

'George Liao,' I said, raising my hands. Wasn't it obvious? He was the only Asian contestant on *The Voice*. 'You know, that guy on *The Voice*?' I added. 'He did a cover of a David Bowie song.'

'Ohhh.' Maggie nodded without meeting my eyes.

A second later, she gasped. 'It's (some Chinese name)!' Maggie's friend squealed. Another tall Asian guy strode onto the stage. With his floppy dark hair and silky shirt, he looked a bit like George Liao too. He waded through ecstatic female cheers and sat down next to the hostess, who had a short pink bob. When he muttered a few words to her, everyone burst out laughing, though I had no clue why.

After the end credits came on, Maggie turned to me again. She asked me all sorts of questions about Melbourne. Did all the houses have swimming pool? How cold was it there? Can you see kangaroos everywhere? That's when I felt a prick on my wrist.

'Ow,' I clutched my arm. 'What's that?'

'Mosquito,' she replied in her high chirpy voice.

'What do I do?'

'Nothing.' She smiled. 'It's just a mosquito.'

'Is it a dengue one?' I'd read about dengue fever. A woman from Sunshine, in Melbourne's west, died from it last year. The mosquito continued buzzing around us with its needle of death. 'Do you have a mosquito patch?'

'What's that?' said Maggie with a frown.

I studied her tilted head, the furrow on her brow. 'Never mind,' I said.

I got up politely and slinked towards the rattan chairs by the window. Tua Teow sat there reading papers. 'What are you reading?' I asked, peering over the large sheet.

Tua Teow lowered the page and I noticed it was all in Mandarin. 'Mudrum pits,' he said glibly.

'What?'

'Mat Rem-pits,' he repeated more slowly. He told me about these motorcycle gangs who went around mugging people in the city. 'There was an accident nearby,' he continued in a whisper. 'The body got cut into half. Want to see?' Tua Teow opened out the paper and shoved it towards me but I quickly shook my head and said, 'No thanks, it's okay.'

I grabbed my sneakers and slipped them on. 'What are you doing?' Tua Teow said, frowning through his glasses.

'Going for a walk,' I replied, lowering my heel into the shoe.

'Where?'

'There's a park down the road, isn't there?'

'Park?' Tua Teow squinted at the sun outside.

'I saw a playground on the way here.'

Tua Teow continued to frown. He looked like he was going to say something but in the end, he just turned back to his newspaper and said, 'Okay.'

* * *

Note to self: Don't take a walk in 30 degrees heat. I'd only been gone about ten minutes and my back was already sticky with sweat. The air here was so dense and heavy, I found it hard to breathe. There was no proper footpath to walk on and all the road names sounded the same—SS5/1, SS5/4, SS5/1A—and they ran in that order too. How did the postman manage to find anything? When I reached a school, I decided to turn back before I got lost.

I strode along the nature strip—if you could call it that. It started off with grass but soon disappeared into patches of gravel. Cars whizzed by so close, I sometimes had to stop to let them pass. As I stepped over a pot-hole, I heard the sound of an engine again, but this time, it didn't pass. It seemed to linger in the distance as if waiting for something. Was it those Mat Rempits Tua Teow had spoken about?

I gripped my handbag and tried to walk calmly. What did Tua Teow say? They grabbed people's bags, dragged them down the street. I pictured gangsters in tattoos, armed with knives and nunchucks. What should I do? Scream, run or call for help? The engine growled, its hot breath rasping at my calf. 'Amoi!' a man called out. He squeaked like a rat and yelled again, 'Amoi!' I was just about to run when I heard the motorbike speed up; only it wasn't a motorbike, it was a car with a man peering out of the passenger window. The car swooshed by and I saw the words emblazoned across the door: POLIS. Police?

When I got back to Tua Ee's house, Roy and Maggie's friends had left. Everyone was bustling around, putting away their cups, getting their bags. 'What's going on?' I said.

'You all ready?' Tua Ee hollered from the kitchen.

'Ready for what?' I asked Maggie.

'We're going for lunch,' she replied.

I took a deep breath. 'Didn't we just have breakfast?'

Chapter 8

Lunch

I soon found out that Tua Ee was serious about food. If it was morning, she would ask what we wanted for lunch. After lunch, she would make plans for dinner and after dinner, she would contemplate the next day's breakfast plans. Lunch, that day, was seafood at the Dragon Boat Palace. However, it was nothing like its namesake on Little Bourke Street. I snapped Dessi a photo of the sign, followed by shots of the outdoor eating area.

The chairs and tables were made of cheap plastic, like swimming pool furniture. A mangy-looking cat was hoovering up scraps of rice from the concrete. There was a faint stench of seaweed coming from either the drain or a rusty pipe near the sink. Tua Ee and company were already making their way towards an indoor section.

I scampered after them and slipped through the glass door. This area was marginally fancier. The tables had tablecloths. There was air-conditioning. Traditional Chinese music wafted in as the tea-cups arrived in a big red basin. Roy picked up a cup and began dousing the other cups with water. As usual, he did not speak to me. He was very polite and responded to my queries about what each dish was. 'Four Seasons with jellyfish salad.' 'Fried fish with plum sauce.' The highlight was the crab—a shiny, vermillion platter whose brethren eyed us from a tank across the room.

Soon, the conversation started to blend into a mix of Hokkien and English. Even when they spoke English, I wasn't sure if it was English. I concentrated on dismantling a crab claw. I dipped my spoon into the soup beside me, a light brown consommé with a lemon inside. I poked at the lemon and sucked the spoon. It didn't quite taste like anything. I smacked my lips and scooped up another spoon.

'What are you doing?' Maggie yelled.

'What?'

She stared at my bowl. 'That's for washing your hands.'

* * *

I gargled for the third time but I could still feel a tickle in my throat. They said it was just Chinese tea but I could taste that faint hint of detergent and something else. I peered into the mirror and saw a bleary-eyed girl with strands of hair sticking to her cheek. The fluorescent light made my cheeks look more sallow and enhanced the circles under my eyes. What was I doing here in this dump of a restroom in the middle of nowhere and was that fungus growing between the tiles?

Roy strode out of the men's toilets. 'You okay?'

'Yeah.'

'The water wasn't dirty,' he assured me. 'I don't think anyone had used it yet.'

The smell of ammonia filled the air. There was no escaping it. 'Are you sure you're okay?' Roy asked.

'Yeah.'

'Do you want some hot tea?'

I shook my head. The thought of tea only made me want to gag. Roy continued to stand there, his hands in his pockets. He shifted his weight from one foot to another. I could feel his gaze

on me. I recalled my manky reflection in the mirror—my damp
face. He must think me so pathetic.

'Do you remember playing with the terrapins at Merlin
Hotel?' he said.

'What?'

'The terrapins,' he repeated. 'At Merlin Hotel. Remember we
used to play there?'

I looked up. A warm feeling grew in my chest as I met
Roy's gaze.

'Yes,' I said quietly.

'I have a picture of us on a bridge,' Roy said with a smile, the
impish smile of his five-year-old self.

I broke into a grin and replied, 'Me too.'

Roy's eyes met mine again and he chuckled. 'You look the
same,' he commented.

'Really?' I recalled the girl in the photo with her two pigtails.

'Yeah,' said Roy. 'Like a chipmunk.'

'A chipmunk!' I exclaimed with a laugh. Roy stuck his teeth
out and I kind of knew what he meant. We spoke about the
Merlin Hotel and the games we used to play. 'Do you remember
the big golden pillars?'

'Yes, the Grand Temple. We had to steal the treasure
from there.'

The fish tank bubbled beside us and the air conditioner
hummed. The tightness in my gut began to disappear and we
began to speak about normal things like what Roy was studying
(accounting) and what he liked to do (football). We both liked
Studio Ghibli films, especially *Spirited Away*.

'That was the best one, right?' he said.

'Definitely.'

'Maggie likes Totoro,' he said, rolling his eyes.

'Oh, I like Totoro too!'

Roy laughed. 'So what do you think of Malaysia?' he asked.

'It's okay.' One of the crabs eyed us from his tank.

'Can I ask you something?' I asked.

'What?'

'Are you angry with me or something?'

Roy's eyes flitted to the Chinese painting on the wall. He said he just felt weird talking to me. 'I don't even understand your accent.'

'I can't understand yours.'

Roy gave me a wry smile. 'I thought you'd be all snooty and stuff but you're actually . . . okay.'

'Thanks. As to your question about what I think of Malaysia: hot, smelly. Not that great.'

'Okay, maybe you are a bit snooty.'

I laughed. 'By the way,' I said. 'What is "Amoi"?' I told him about the police car incident from earlier.

'Amoi means Chinese girl.'

Chinese girl, is that what I looked like to them? I thought of the sea of people I had seen at the airport. All the patrons in the restaurant. Everyone had dark hair like me, except for that little granny in the corner with a silvery head. I guess I did look like everyone here but for some reason, I didn't feel like them at all.

Not long after, we all gathered outside, full and overfed. When Pa and I reached Tua Ee's Honda, Maggie skipped over to me. 'What are you going to do now?'

'Go back to the house?'

'Do you want to come with us to Pete's place?'

I wracked my brain trying to remember who Pete was. Had I met him just now?

'We'll be back before dinner,' said Maggie.

To be honest, I was hot and sweaty. I just wanted to go back and switch on the aircon. 'Yes Katie,' said Pa, jumping in. 'Why don't you go? I have quite a few things to sort out today. You can go spend time with your cousins.'

I turned to Maggie and shrugged. 'Okay,' I said.

Chapter 9

Pete's Place

'Pete's Place' was actually a place called 'Pete's Place'. It looked like some kind of restaurant on the first floor of a shopping strip. Downstairs was a pharmacy and an Indian shop selling tosai, and up a narrow flight of stairs was Pete's Place, or at least that's what the sign said.

Roy and Maggie pushed open the door and a high-pitched sound pierced the air. Groups of people ebbed and flowed, and when the crowd parted, I made out a stage at the end of the room. 'What is this place?' I asked. 'Some kind of bar?

'Sort of,' Maggie replied. 'But we're here to watch some bands.'

Roy found us a table at the back and went off to talk to some friends. He seemed to have a lot of friends here. Maggie and I sat down and watched some people setting up the stage. Maggie glanced at her watch. 'It might take a while. I think the next gig is only on in fifteen minutes.'

'That's okay,' I said, whipping out my bag.

'What is that?' exclaimed Maggie. 'Are you reading a Maths book?' She gestured to the book I was holding.

'It's a log book,' I said.

'You're reading it?' Maggie snatched the book from me and flipped through the pages.

'Yeah, I'm memorizing the logarithms,' I said. Was it not obvious? If you knew them by heart, you'd be so much quicker on tests. Maggie laughed and handed the book back to me. 'I've never seen anyone memorize a log book before.'

A mike squealed from the stage. 'Oh, they're starting,' said Maggie. It was a Chinese band singing a Mandarin song. The lead singer was a skinny boy with glasses who looked more like he belonged in a science lab, yet there he was, rocking away like Anthony Kiedis. (I know Anthony Kiedis because Dessi was once obsessed with the Red Hot Chilli Peppers.) When he got to the chorus, the guy switched to a line of English—'Do you know it's me? Do you know it's me?'—and this line kept running through my head even when they moved on to other songs.

After they finished, four guys came onto the stage. The singer had a slick updo like this Italian boy from St Patricks' a lot of girls admired. The bass guitarist looked a bit like Roy. I was going to tell Maggie that when she stood up and cheered, 'Woo-hoo!'

'Is that Roy?' I exclaimed.

'Yea-ah!' she replied, clapping her hands. Indeed, he was no longer talking to the guy at the bar. Maggie pointed out Leong on guitar, Kit on drums and the guy singing in the centre was Shang. They all looked vaguely familiar and I realized they might have been at Tua Khor's house earlier that day.

They did a Foo Fighters cover. Then a couple of other numbers Dessi would probably have classified as 'postmodern elliptical garage'. After they finished, another band came on. My attention wandered to the posters on the wall—advertisements for things like coconut juice and something called FM18. There were like ten of them in a row. 'What is that?' I said. 'A radio station?'

'No, FM stands for Free Malaysia.' Maggie described the event as a concert to enact change, a rebellion against the forces of evil. I thought she was joking but her voice continued to be serious. 'Have you heard of the Wira group?' she said.

'Yeah.' I recalled Pa talking about them before, probably in one of his political rants which I often failed to pay attention to.

'Ever since they came into power, they've been banning everything. We used to have heaps of concerts and gigs but they've all been cancelled.'

'Why?'

'Apparently it's "death metal" and "corrupting the nation's youth".'

'Is it?'

'Of course not! It's stuff like this.' She gestured at a band playing Maroon 5. 'We've had enough and we're going to change things. The FM18 will be the first proper gig we've had in years.'

'Who is "we"?'

'All of us.' She pointed towards the stage. 'Most of the people here are practising for the concert. It's organized by Pete and this is one of the few places you can play anyway.'

'Who's Pete?'

'Oh, he's the white guy over there; he owns the place.'

* * *

And so that's how I came to know about Pete and this eclectic bunch. Boys in oversized Nirvana T-shirts, girls with nails the colour of electricity. During a break, we sat down in a circle at the back of the room. Shang started plucking his bass guitar. Another guy started beating a bongo. At first, it was just random sounds. Then Roy joined in with a lead guitar riff and somehow, it became a song. Towards the end, everything got faster and louder and more intense, then Roy let out a final strum and laughter rang around the room.

'Hey Katie.' Roy turned to me. 'Do you play anything?'

'No, not really.'

'You play the guitar, right?' said Maggie. 'I heard you play classical guitar. Can you play us something?'

'No . . .'

'Leong, pass her a guitar,' said Roy.

'No, I'm not very—'

Someone thrust a guitar into my hands.

I had no choice. I chose the song from my school audition, Vivaldi's Concerto in D. As always, I stumbled along with stilted fingers. When I reached the thrill bit, it only got worse but I forced myself to charge through, to swim through this underwater tunnel, until I reached the end.

When I lowered the guitar, the whole room was quiet. It was like the world had stopped. The only sound I could hear was my heart pounding slowly. 'That was good,' said Roy. He looked at Maggie; Maggie tugged at her earring. Then, everyone started talking about the FM18.

* * *

He looked at me from the other end of the room. He had been looking since I put the guitar down. It's funny what you can grasp in a second. Long curly hair, a strong, sharp jawline. There were two others with him—a guy and a girl. The three of them had this quality about them, that made them seem like people who were different. Maybe it was their dusky skin or the way they acted; like they didn't care what anyone thought of them.

The girl flicked back her long dark hair. The guy whipped out his guitar. 'Who are they?' I asked Maggie.

'What?'

'Those people over there.'

'Don't look,' she whispered. 'I think they're looking at us.'

It was hard not to look. Especially at the guy with the curly hair. There was something particularly beautiful about his features. I couldn't place his race; Mexican, Japanese, Italian—a mix of all three? I just wanted to keep staring and drink up his beauty but I forced myself to focus on the counter in front of me, on the specks on the counter, and a coaster that said 'Malaysia Boleh'.

In the end, I went to the bar and ordered a lime juice. 'That will be four fifty,' said the cashier. I peered into my wallet trying to pick out the right change. Was that a ringgit? I couldn't remember what it looked like. One of the coins fell out and rolled onto the floor. As I searched for it, a hand came out and handed it to me.

'Oh, thanks,' I said. I found myself staring into the face of the curly-haired boy. He had the kind of eyes you couldn't help staring at because they looked so bright, like there were hundreds of thoughts going off in his head.

'You should have enough there,' he said, pointing to the notes in my hand.

'Oh, yeah.' I forgot two ringgit here came in notes.

The guy continued to stare at me. 'You look familiar,' he said. 'Have we met before?'

'I don't think so. I just arrived.'

'No, you've been here awhile. I saw you come in.' A warm flush swept over me and I gripped my wallet more tightly.

'As in . . . from the airport,' I stammered.

'Where are you from?' the boy asked.

I cleared my throat. 'Australia,' I said softly.

'I see.'

My face grew hot under his gaze. 'Hi!' a waitress waved at him from the other end of the counter. He strode over and began talking to her. I watched her light up as she took his order. He smiled, she laughed and stared after him as he walked away. I wished Dessi was there. He looked like the kind of guy who would have a theme song and she would know exactly what it would be.

The bartender grabbed a lime and deftly sliced it into quarters. His knife made juicy, sharp sounds on the board. Roy emerged from the restrooms and was about to say hi, when a guy walked up to him—the same guy with the soft, dark curls. The guy did a

quick scan of the room including me in it, thought I don't think
he registered me there. He had this way of looking at things as if
he were processing everything in his head in a single glance—the
dance floor, the bar, the foyer—tabulating whatever he saw in that
brain of his.

'You guys are early,' Roy said stiffly.

'I didn't know there was a set time,' replied the guy.

'What are you doing here?'

'Playing.'

'Are you trying to stop us?'

'Of course not.'

The guy stood up straighter. Whatever he said next, made Roy
fold his arms. The guy narrowed his eyes. He was an inch taller
than Roy.

'Lime juice?' called out the bartender.

'Oh, thanks.' When I turned around, the two guys had
disappeared. The black curtains shivered slightly to the sounds of
some Indie drums.

I got back to the table and found everyone packing up. 'What's
going on?' I said.

'We're going,' replied Maggie.

'I thought they had one more set.'

She glanced at Roy. 'They had a bit of a fight.'

'Who?'

The beautiful guy with curly hair was staring at me again.

'Don't look,' whispered Maggie. I gripped my drink. Did he
just realize I was with them? Had Roy seen me talking to him?
I took a sip from my glass and pushed it away.

'You ready?' said Roy, his guitar case in hand.

'Yep,' I said, grabbing my bag.

The others were all standing up as well. I strode with them across
the dance floor, following the click of Maggie's heels. Somewhere
in the middle, we crossed paths with the guy and his friends. They
walked past. I walked past, flanked by the footsteps of my cousins.

Chapter 10

Funeral

I forgot how hot it could be. It didn't help that I was wearing black. The ivory casket lay in the centre of the living room, cool and shiny amidst the warmth of mourners shuffling in and out. The standing fan in the corner provided minor relief. It blew in the smell of perfume and perspiration, from jackets buttoned a little too tightly; dresses, stiff and fitted.

Ah Ma had passed away while she was sleeping in her TV chair. Everyone said it was a good way to go. I examined the picture of the woman on the easel: pink lips, short curly hair. The woman beneath the glass looked the same. The only thing I could remember about Ah Ma was that she always wore *samfus*. I don't remember speaking to her or doing anything with her but I have this image of a woman in a samfu pantsuit. Sometimes they were floral, sometimes plain and sometimes a little shiny for special occasions—but it was always that matching top and bottom design.

That's what she was wearing right now. I could tell through the glass. She was wearing a lilac samfu top with a shiny trim in a deeper lilac, her hands crossed over her chest in a peaceful and demure manner. It struck me that this was the first time I was seeing a dead person. I was not sure what to do. I took a step forward and bowed my head as if in prayer. I stood there long enough to notice the jade ring on Ah Ma's finger and that the casket had very pretty gold hinges.

Five more seconds should be enough. I took a step back. Everyone seemed wrapped up in their little clusters. A lady in a black *cheongsam*, two men huddled together. It was as if everyone fit where they were supposed to; everyone except me.

I slinked away to the kitchen where woks and pots hung around me like in an old forest. A distant crowd hummed. 'You can just put it there,' he said.

'What?'

'Your cup.'

The boy gestured towards a counter littered with plastic cups. 'What are you doing?' he asked.

'Clearing my plate?'

'I can do that.'

I noticed then his waiter-black pants and his white shirt. 'Oh, thanks,' I said, handing him my plate. I went up to a jug and poured myself a drink. 'What is this?' I said, examining the little white beads inside.

'Barley, haven't you had it before?'

I shook my head.

'That was an interesting song you played yesterday,' he stated.

My head snapped up. 'Oh, it's you.'

His long curly hair was tied back in a ponytail but it was definitely the same guy from Pete's Place. His eyebrows were dark and defined. His eyes still as bright and laughing as they were yesterday. 'I'm not supposed to talk to you,' I said.

'Why?'

'Roy wouldn't like it. He's my cousin.'

'I see.'

The boy didn't seem to care. 'I'm Justin,' he said. A lock of hair fell upon his jaw. His lips were full and red.

'Katie,' I mumbled.

A gust of air blew in from the living room and I frowned at the crowd, milling around like sheep. This was the human race. Their voices merged into that respectable hum that only the dead or the very old could conjure. 'Are you related to . . .' Justin gestured towards the coffin.

'She was my grandmother.'

'I'm sorry.'

'It's okay, I was not that close to her.'

I continued to stare at the coffin in the next room. *What had hers looked like?* Was it creamy white like this or maybe a warm wood timber? Had there been many flowers?

'You sure you're okay?' Justin asked.

'Yes, I was just thinking about my mum, actually. She passed away when I was young.' Justin nodded and placed another plate into a bucket. I didn't know this guy but there was something about him that made me feel comfortable. He picked up another plate and emptied its contents into the bin.

'I'm trying to recall the funeral,' I said, 'but I don't remember anything. It's not like they have photos of these things, right?'

'How old were you then?'

'About seven, I think, but she was here in Malaysia when it happened. I was in Melbourne.'

Justin wiped his hands on his apron. 'How did she die?'

'Pneumonia. A lot of people die from it, you know. Usually you're sick with something else but then the bacteria gets into your lungs. You think it's just a cough but it's actually these germs attacking your lungs and filling them up with water. One day, you start coughing, the next day you're dead. It's like drowning.'

'Oh . . . is that what happened?'

'Yes, I read it on the Internet.'

Justin's mouth tweaked into a small smile. He turned away and started stacking some cups. Truth was, mum probably died because she was overtired. Pneumonia is usually just the by-product of something deeper. She probably had pre-existing conditions that were the real cause of her death. I should know, of all people. I recalled that day in the kitchen, her shopping all over the floor.

'What's wrong?' asked Justin again.

'Nothing. It's quite nice out here, away from everyone.'

'Yeah.'

I sat down on the doorstep and a bird darted out of the hedge. There was something calming about the green leaves in front of me and the hardness of the concrete under my feet. It felt warm and safe, as if I was connected to the centre of the earth. My phone buzzed with a message. It was John Ichuda asking me how I was. I took a photo of the bird in the hedge and sent it to him. He 'hearted' it and sent back a picture of a tennis court filled with puddles.

John Ichuda : **Raining and 12 degrees here. Must be so nice and warm there.**

Me : **It's a bit too warm. I'd prefer the 12 degrees.**

'Who's that?' said Justin, looking amused. 'Your boyfriend?'

'No, why?'

'Just the way you were smiling.'

'Just a friend,' I said lightly. I wouldn't consider John Ichuda a boyfriend—yet. We hadn't broached the subject at all and our conversations had remained strictly platonic so far.

'Do you have a boyfriend?' Justin asked.

'No.' I'm not sure if I've ever had a boyfriend unless you considered Ryan White, whom I went to the Year 10 formal with. We snuck a kiss behind the venue only because we were all dressed-up and feeling curious. We saw each other at the library the following week and completely ignored each other.

I checked my phone again but John Ichuda had not replied. When I looked up, Justin was squinting at me. 'Are you Chinese?' he asked.

'Yeah, why?'

'You don't look Chinese.'

I chuckled. 'You are the first person to say that.' I thought of all my school photos over the years, I was often the only Chinese person in class. The chink. Fart girl. The one with the weird dad who packed her a hard-boiled egg which stank up the whole classroom.

I watched the laundry flapping on the line. Nothing unrespectable. They were just ordinary dishcloths and towels of various sizes but they reminded me of the joy of walking through fresh, clean sheets; the shapes they made on the ground. I remembered thinking that each shadow was a block of safety and I had to jump from one block to another. There is a wonderful sense of comfort being wrapped up in the scent of hot, clean clothes, which is almost like a hug. This is what I wrote when one of the psychologists asked me to jot down my best memories of her. I remembered white sheets flapping hot on the line; I remember the hem of her skirt as she reached up for a peg.

Justin carried the basin outside and placed it under the tap. There was a leanness about him that veered on skinny if not for his shoulders, that I knew were broad from the way his shirt stretched across his back. Baggy sleeves flapped over his elbows and a line rippled along his forearm when he turned off the tap. He came and sat down beside me, fishing for something in his pocket. 'Want one?' He held out a spearmint stick.

'No thanks.' I offered him a bottle of Blackmores.

'Nah, I don't do drugs.'

'It's Vitamin C!'

He smiled and shook his head. The both of us sat there, looking at the hedge. There were little red berries between the cracks and a faint scent of tea tree oil.

We spoke about random things like birds in Malaysia versus birds in Melbourne. Pa and Diana. 'Hang on,' said Justin. 'You call your dad's friend Diana?'

'Yeah, why?'

'I can't imagine calling any of my parents' friends by their first names. Or my friends' parents, for that matter.'

'What do you call them then?'

'Aunty or Uncle—it's a sign of respect. Like Aunty Molly or Uncle Hamid.'

When I met Diana, she wasn't quite Pa's friend. More of mine, I suppose, if you consider a psychologist a friend. She'd introduced herself as Diana, so it would be weird to call her anything else. And Dessi's mum? No, I think Sarah would be offended if I called her Aunty Sarah! Might make her feel old.

* * *

A mike squeaked from inside the house. Both Justin and I turned to look. Pa was talking to the priest. Funny how small he looked as he nodded and frowned at the floor. Maybe it was the way his arms were folded or maybe I had grown bigger. He caught me looking and lifted his arm in an awkward wave.

'Is that your dad?' said Justin.

'Yes, why?' I studied his expression for a second longer. 'Do you know him?'

'No,' said Justin quickly. He fiddled with his glass and said, 'You guys don't look that alike.'

'Really? Some people say we do.' I had Pa's bone structure, his rounded nose, his sharp chin, an overall resemblance. I wondered what Justin saw. He took a sip from his glass and said, 'What does he do in Melbourne?'

'Pa? He works at a biscuit factory.'

'Interesting.'

'Really? Sounds pretty boring to me but the pay is pretty good for what they do. He gets off work by three.'

Justin frowned and fiddled with his glass again. 'Does he do anything else?'

'What do you mean?'

'Does he do any other work?'

'Ah, ok.' Yes, I knew what he meant. Jessica Coleman's dad owned a real estate company. And Anya Gill's dad was a partner at a law firm. Pa . . . worked in a biscuit factory. 'No,' I said. 'I don't think so. Maybe some share market stuff. He's always on his computer. I know, it's pretty lame, isn't it?'

Justin gasped. 'No, no, I didn't mean that at all. I was just curious, maybe he had a hobby or something.'

I let on a wry grin. 'Nope. He works at Arnott's . . . packing biscuits . . . into a tin.' I smiled, simulating the packing motions with my hands.

When I grew up, I planned to be a doctor. Anya's mum was a cardiologist and I saw how respectful people became when they heard this. You could see it in their faces. That's what I was going to do. But first, scholarship class, get into a good school and then a f#@king good ATAR.

Justin was folding something with his hands—a chewing gum wrapper. He folded it one way and then another, and then it became a tight square. I watched his fingers dance around its edges, waiting to see what it would turn into next. As it started to get all pointy, a voice boomed over our heads.

'What are you doing?' said Tua Ee. 'Why are you sitting on the floor like that?'

'I was just—'

'I was looking for you everywhere. Come on, there's someone I want you to meet.'

Justin got up and returned to the tap area. I stood up, flicking the dust off my skirt.

* * *

She introduced me to a group of people as 'Paul's daughter from Melbourne'. I forgot their names as soon as I heard them. They spoke about how pretty I was and how rosy my cheeks were, while Tua Ee basked in the praise. We moved from the living room to the front terrace and then to the garden, chatting with different groups along the way—and the same thing repeated until everything became somewhat of a blur.

My face ached from smiling. I slid under a palm tree and stood in its pear-shaped shadow. People continued to bustle around like atoms trying to find molecules to attach to, before changing positions again. As a cool breeze blew, a stylish-looking lady slipped next to me. 'Hi,' she said, looking immaculate in a fitted black dress. A pair of earrings dangled from her ears, bearing jewels the colour of a lake, switching from green to clear.

'Hi,' I said, re-donning my smile. The lady was like a collection of angles. From the way she tilted her hip to the way her bob sliced her jaw. 'Sorry, did we meet before? Tua Ee has been introducing me to so many people.'

The lady laughed. She said Tua Ee would not have introduced her. Her name was Lily. She liked my dress. 'Is it Kate Spade? It looks very Kate Spade.'

'No, just Target . . . a department store in Australia,' I added.

'Oh, I know it,' Lily replied.

She took a sip of wine and suspended her glass between two fingers. 'You look so much like your mother,' she stated.

I turned to look at her, taking in her light smile and shining eyes. 'You knew my mother?'

'Yes, I see her quite often.'

The world began to spin around me. It was as though Mrs Jarvis, my science teacher, was suddenly telling me, 'The world is flat, didn't you know?' Lily continued speaking as if she were talking about the weather. 'Well, maybe not so often these days,' she drawled. 'We are all so busy.'

I tightened my hand into a fist and said, 'My mother passed away, a long time ago.'

Lily tilted her head to one side. 'Really?'

She clamped her mouth shut, looking like she was holding things back. She then relaxed into a smile. 'I've heard a lot about you,' she said, her eyes soft. 'I wasn't sure whether to come but I'm glad I caught you.'

'What do you mean?'

Lily looked distracted by something across the room. 'Let's talk more tomorrow,' she said in a quiet voice. She scanned her dress as if looking for something. Her eyelids gleamed with silver eye shadow, the wine twinkled in her glass. 'Now where did I put it?' She switched her drink from her left hand to her right and fumbled deep into her clutch. 'Meet me here,' she mumbled, handing me a plain white envelope.

'What?' I asked.

'Tomorrow,' she murmured. 'Maybe around noon?'

'Lily,' exclaimed Tua Ee. She swooped in in her voluminous black dress. 'Didn't expect to see you here.'

'Oh, why not?'

'Aren't you supposed to be in Canada?' Tua Ee stared at Lily, eyebrows fiercely auburn. Lily stared back without flinching.

'Yes, we're leaving next week.'

'Wonderful,' said Tua Ee. Their voices seemed extra brittle in the late morning sun. Smiles a little too wide. Lily drained her glass and directed her gaze at Tua Ee. 'Well, I should get going then. My condolences.' She gave a bow that was so long and slow that

I thought she might topple over. 'Aunty Margaret was always very kind to Suzanna and myself. Her butter cookies were legendary.'

She pronounced the word 'legendary' like royalty but it was the name she uttered before that which pricked my ears.

'Oh, look at the time,' she announced. 'I should really get going. It was nice to meet you, my dear,' said Lily to me. 'Hopefully, we'll meet again.' She cast me a meaningful look and spun off.

Tua Ee and I watched her sashay towards the house. When she disappeared into the crowd, I said, 'What was she talking about?'

'What do you mean?' Tua Ee scanned the garden as if she was busy looking for something.

'Which Suzanna did she mean?' I prodded.

'I don't know, I didn't hear. Did you see how much she was drinking?' Tua Ee muttered about how no one invited Lily to parties. She was always causing a scene. She's been like that since her husband had left her. Lucky that her daughter wanted Lily to go to Canada with her. 'Oh, they're starting the prayers soon,' Tua Ee proclaimed as she peered into the house. I couldn't see anything but she quickly steered me to the door. Throughout the twenty-four Hail Marys, Our Fathers and Glory Bes, a constant thought rang though my head: *What was Lily talking about? Was it really just nonsense?*

Chapter 11

The Morning After

I woke up the next morning to a low rumbling sound. It sounded like a tram on Bourke Street—then I remembered where I was. Honey-coloured sun transformed the daisies on the curtain into a field of gold. A crack of light lit up the parquet floor. On the wall, the air conditioner rumbled—it was one of those wooden systems you had to switch on and off directly from the unit. It faintly smelled of cloves thanks to the scented anti-bacterial spray I had used on it on the day we'd arrived.

I wriggled my toes at the bottom of the waffle-weave blanket and soaked up the atmosphere of the rest of the room, imagining myself as the child who had lived here before. I wondered if it was Roy or Maggie. There was a porcelain cross above the dresser with the words, 'God, please bless this room' written on it.

Blu tac marks shone on the wall, presumably holding up posters from a bygone time, maybe Bananarama and Totoro, like what I had in my room before. A motorcycle tooted outside, jarring me out of my haze. The events of the funeral yesterday came back to me. Lily. Tua Ee. Had it all been a dream?

No, the envelope was still there on the bedside table. I opened the flap and took the photo out. There was Pa in sideburns, looking twenty years younger, a mug of beer in his hands. Lily stood beside him, equally cheery. But it was the woman on the right I couldn't stop looking at.

She had her back to the camera, so all I could see were her hands on her hips, the shadow of her smile. A big hat was blocking her face so I couldn't completely make out her features. I drilled into the image, wishing I could tilt the camera or move her hat but I suppose it was enough. From the tilt of her head and the curve of her cheek, I could tell she was laughing.

I turned the photo over, hoping to find more than the few words at the back. But that's all there was: 'Villa Kemboja, Kampung Damai, September 1976.' Kem-bo-*ja*. *Kem*–bo-ja? How did you even pronounce it? The small, neat handwriting flew across the page, flicking up perfectly at the end of each word. Was she really alive?

I stuffed the photo back into the envelope and went to my dresser. Check temperature. Check teeth. My dresser top looked exactly the way it did in Melbourne. Toner, moisturizer, toilet case. The arrangement of these items filled me with a sense of ease as the world outside churned away in all its unpredictability.

When I went down to the kitchen, I found Siti washing the dishes. Siti was always working—washing the dishes, peeling onions, chopping chicken. She wiped a wok dry and hung it up on a hook alongside the other pots and pans hanging above the sink. When she saw me, she smiled and headed outside, a laundry basket pressed against her hip.

'Morning,' Pa said, looking up from the kitchen table. I hadn't seen him there, sitting in the corner.

'You going out?' I said, noting his slacks and shirt.

'Yeah, I've got to meet some lawyers later. Did you sleep okay?'

'Yeah, you?'

'Yeah.' He started packing up the papers strewn in front of him.

'What's that?'

'It's just the estate stuff.'

'Do you need help?' I reached out for a pile.

'No, no, it's fine.' He shuffled the papers up and shoved them into a manila folder. There was no trace of the laughing man from the picture.

'Hey,' I said, clearing my throat. 'Can I ask you something?'

'Will it take long?'

'No, I just wanted to—'

Pa narrowed his eyes at me and sighed. I'd seen that look before. He was afraid I was going to ask him something he couldn't answer, afraid of not knowing what to say. Most of the time, I didn't really need him to say anything, to be honest, I just wanted him to listen. 'I'm in a bit of a rush. Can we talk later?' He pinched his lip. 'We'll meet for dinner tonight, okay?' Pa grabbed his bag, he grabbed his phone, then at the kitchen door, he paused. 'You okay?'

'Yeah.'

'Tua Ee will be back after lunch,' he said. 'Maybe you can do something with her first?'

'Okay.'

Pa remained standing at the door. 'What are you going to do?'

'I've got some schoolwork to do.'

Pa frowned at the light coming through the window. It lit up the pots and pans hanging from the hooks and washed over his face, accentuating his tanned skin and the dent on his forehead. 'Okay,' he said and left.

In the silence of the kitchen, I studied the clean countertop, no longer covered with plates and cups from the funeral party. The sink was spotless save for the bright yellow washcloth Siti had wrung and placed to dry in between the two sinks. Outside, a wet bedsheet flapped in the wind alongside a row of large women's undergarments, all in the same nude shade. I glanced at my feet and spotted a piece of paper on the floor. Was that one of Pa's receipts? The yellow slip said 'Mentari. Vote for change.' Nothing on the back. I squinted at the words and popped it back onto the table.

Chapter 12

Taxi

I called a taxi at 10.50 a.m. Lily had said to meet at noon, so that would be plenty of time. Every time a car drove past, I peered through the door grille to look. First, it was the opposite neighbour's car. Next, it was some silver car that didn't even stop. Finally, a red-and-white Proton pulled up to the gate.

I checked the number plate and saw that it matched the number the lady at the taxi company had given me. The moment I slid into the backseat, the smell of something sweet hit me— Floral Orange, I gathered from the pot of fragrance next to the driver. He squinted at the piece of paper I handed him. '*Dekat Pasar Seni, kah?*'

'Sorry, do you speak English?' I said.

'Oh, you not Malaysian?'

I shook my head.

'Kampung Damai . . .' he said, reading the words. 'Near Central Market?'

'I think so,' I said, not very sure at all. When I googled Kampung Damai, it said 'Kampung' meant 'Village' and Kampung Damai was one of the only Malay villages left in the city.

The man turned back to the steering wheel. The picture on the dashboard showed a clean-shaven man with dark, drilling eyes. But the man driving had a goatee. The hand that clutched the gear box flashed a gold ring, and a white skull-cap adorned his head. His identification card said his name was Mohammad bin Ehsan. Was that really him? What if it wasn't? I thought of those Mat Rempits Uncle Patrick was telling me about—those gangsters on bikes— or maybe this guy was a terrorist. He looked just like Osama bin Laden—or what I thought Osama bin Laden might look like.

I messaged Dessi, silently snapping a picture of the guy's dashboard.

Me : **Hey. I'm in a taxi. The driver looks dodgy. If I go missing, this is his ID.**

Dessi : ☺

Me : **I'm serious. I can just sense that he may be dangerous.**

Dessi : **Okay**

Mohammad bin Ehsan stopped at the traffic light and fiddled with the radio buttons. Bits of Malay music sprang out as he flicked through various channels. Was he really taking me to Villa Kemboja? Was this how kidnappings happened? He paused at a station where a man began rattling away in Malay, before moving on to something else.

I clutched my bag, ready to spring out. Finally, a familiar tinkle of piano notes streamed out of the speakers and Mohammad bin Ehsan turned around. 'You like?' he grinned. 'Richard Marx.' He tapped his steering wheel and sung along to '*Right Here Waiting*', mouthing every single word until the end. We sat through a few other English songs, such as 'Country Roads, Take Me Home' and 'Saturday Night Fever'. As Olivia Newton John's 'Xanadu' came to an end, Mohammad bin Ehsan stopped the car and let me out. 'Over there,' he said, pointing to the right.

* * *

For a moment, I didn't see anything, just rows of office towers gleaming in the sun. The Petronas Twin Towers, two silver rockets shooting out like in the brochures, then across the road, I saw the wooden huts balancing on stilts. They rested between coconut trees like dinosaurs grazing with their necks outstretched, oblivious to the glitter and glamour that surrounded them. What was this village doing in the middle of nowhere?

A pair of school girls hung from a fence and stared at me. They wore long white hijabs that reached down to their knees. As I walked by, I could feel their gazes following me, examining my linen dress, my flushed cheeks, wondering why I wasn't wearing a headscarf. I drifted past a grocery store with straw brooms outside. A post office. Street stalls selling bananas, cakes, trays of beaded jewellery in bright plastic baskets.

When I reached the end of the street, two men stepped out. Were they police? I squinted at the crescent logos on their shirt pockets. The tubbier older man pointed at me and muttered something in Malay. The younger man clasped the baton on his hip. Was he going to hit me? I took a step back, the sun piercing my eyes, and out of this glare, a figure blocked out the light.

Justin stepped into the scene like some kind of apparition, in a glittery gold top. He spoke to the two men in a soft, calm voice that reminded me of Gandalf casting a spell. He pointed at the trees and gestured back at me. They frowned. But when he pushed away his soft curls and smiled, the men smiled back and even broke out into a laugh.

'What did they say?' I asked after they left.

'This is a mosque area,' said Justin. 'You can't wear that.'

'Wear what?' I looked down at my sandals.

Justin pointed at a sign on the wall. I scanned the symbols and crosses. No thongs, no swimwear, no tank tops . . . Was it my dress? It was a just a shift dress, hardly indecent, but I supposed it didn't have sleeves. Justin took out a checked shirt from his bag and handed it to me. I put it on and the scent of fresh laundry enveloped me. It held the same magic as from my childhood, but the scent was different, a concoction from a different forest—spicier, brighter, with a trace of citrus.

Suddenly, I was privy to Justin's secrets—his bedroom, his house, the smell of his home. I showed him the address of the villa and he said he knew the place but we had to go around the mosque. 'Where is the mosque?' I asked, peering around. He pointed towards the bushes as he had done earlier, and this time, I saw the tip of a blue dome peering above the trees. When I narrowed my eyes, I could even make out the glisten of other blue domes from in-between the leaves.

As Justin and I walked back through the market, people did not stare as much. It was as if his shirt had made me invisible. 'Do you normally wear that?' I gestured to his shiny top.

'I was at the mosque.'

'You go often?'

'Not really, I was just accompanying my father.'

Other people walked by, wearing similar shiny tops. Mostly men, hurrying across the road or getting into their cars. I saw the two men who had stopped me earlier, further down the street. 'Are they police?' I asked Justin, gesturing towards them.

'Wira police,' he replied.

'What does that mean?'

'They are all volunteers, but you need to listen to them if you are here. You shouldn't be walking around by yourself.'

'Why? I walk around by myself all the time in Melbourne.'

He stopped. 'This isn't Melbourne.' A motorbike chugged by, carrying two youth without helmets. They zipped dangerously down a lane.

We walked past houses older and bigger than the ones I had seen before. Their gardens were large and leafy. They emanated a sense of age and grandeur simply by having been around in the world longer, standing tall and proud, as if saying, 'I've been here longer than you, I've seen more than you'll ever see.'

They reminded me of those mansions on Toorak Road despite just being made of wood.

Justin and I walked until we reached a black iron gate. 'This is it,' he announced. Long dark shadows stretched over a driveway covered with leaves. An amber butterfly flitted through the bars. 'What's wrong?' he asked.

'It's so beautiful,' I whispered. The black-and-white photo had not revealed the colours of the house. The turquoise steps, the yellow eaves, a front door awash in pink. It was as if the painter had tried to pluck the most unlikely combinations he could think of, the result of which was this splash of brilliance.

Justin said he had to go and left me standing there. A leaf teetered in the bushes, another butterfly appeared. Then I saw the cat. It slinked behind a bamboo plant, only to emerge again on the other side. 'Hey Cat,' I said, reaching out to it. It continued to observe me the way cats do, giving me the side-eye, looking at me over its nose. The moment I opened the gate, however, it scurried away.

A flock of sparrows flew up as I crept towards the house. Leaves crunched under my sandals. The porch steps had the most beautiful tile. A crimson petunia, a, deep-blue daisy—each a work of art so beautiful, I hesitated to step on it. Then I reached the door. Pink like in *Hansel and Gretel* and window shutters the colour of lime. My heart sped up as I noticed the vines crawling up the wall—exactly like in the photo.

'Lily?' I called out. 'Hello?' I knocked on the door. The sound dissipated into the shadows but nothing else moved. There was neither rustle nor creak as the soft wind blew. I noticed half a dozen pots on the deck, each with seedlings inside, in different stages of growth; a bucket with a shovel; a pair of gloves on top with mandarin prints, still orange and sunny despite the sprinkle of dirt. After what seemed like an hour, I made my way back down. The garden was a crazed concoction of bougainvillea, ferns and tropical leaves with splashes of maroon. In the middle of it all, the banana tree stood slightly stooped with the weight of about a hundred fruit on it. I smiled and snapped a picture for Dessi and just as I did, a voice broke through the air.

'Who are you?' she said. Her blouse fluttered in the wind. Her hair was twisted into a low bun, a single strand fluttering at her cheek. In that light, the way she was looking at me, I knew exactly who she was.

Part III

Kampung Damai

Chapter 13

And So We Meet

'Is Lily here?' I asked.

'No.'

The lady frowned, a light furrow denting the smooth skin of her forehead. My heart began to race and words began to jumble up in my head but I forced myself to calm down. 'Breathe, Katie,' I imagined Diana saying. 'It's all in your mind.'

'Are you . . . Suzanna?' The name felt brittle on my tongue.

'Yes . . . and you are?'

'I'm Katie.'

I watched my name sink into this person, into this lady standing in front of me in a green *baju kurung*, a scarf around her hair. She tilted her head to one side and her honey-brown skin gleamed in the sun, shades darker than mine. 'You are Malay?' I sputtered.

'Um-hm.' She nodded and let me inside.

I followed her into the kitchen, my eyes fixed on her wispy green blouse, the colour of the lorikeets in our garden. It explained so many things. How my hair was wavy unlike any other Chinese girl in school; my eyes that were much larger than Pa's.

'Lily didn't say anything about you coming,' mused Suzanna. 'Let me call her . . .' She waited a few seconds, and then another few. 'She's not picking up.' Suzanna punched out a message. 'She told me you were here,' she said, eyes still on her phone.

'You knew I was here . . .' I muttered.

'Yes.' She continued to avoid my gaze. She offered me a chair at the table. 'Would you like some tea? It's lemongrass, from the garden.'

That voice, that voice. No, I did not remember it. A bangle twirled down, bright gold against the darkness of her skin. Had she worn this before? Had she worn any jewellery before? It was so quiet I could hear every chink and chime in the room. 'You think it's going to rain?' she continued. 'I hope it does. It will be good for the plants.' Gossamer curtains fluttered on the windows. Gossamer. Gossamer like my blue dress, except these were white. Suzanna pottered around the kitchen, her long skirt swishing at the ankles. I had a flashback of her in our kitchen, making me Milo; playing beside her in the garden as she watered the plants.

I lie. I remembered none of this. She handed me a cup and sat down at the marble table, opposite me. 'You have been here before, you know,' she explained. 'This was your grandfather's house.' The gossamer curtains whispered like ladies in the corner. Had I been here before? I examined the shelves filled with leatherbound books. A table fan turning. 'It's so hot, isn't it?' Suzanna said, removing her scarf. She unclipped her hair and reclipped it—but not before I saw it tumble down in waves, just the way mine did when I combed it at night.

A cat slinked between the chair legs, the cat from before. 'This is Encik Nasir,' Suzanna said, scooping him up.

'Encik . . . is that Mister?'

'Yes, so he is Mister Nasir,' she said, looking at the cat and smiling.

There was a regal quality about him with his grand white whiskers but it was his orange stripes that made me stare. 'We have a cat like that in my neighbourhood,' I said. 'He even has that same triangular marking on his head.'

'Really?' said Suzanna, smiling like a cat herself. She asked me how Melbourne was and I said it was spring there now.

'Ah,' she mused, as if she remembered. 'Do you still go to the playground on the hill? I suppose not. You are too old for playgrounds.'

The heat of the mug grew in my hand. 'They told me you died.'

Suzanna pursed her lips and nodded. A heavy silence weighed down the room. 'I felt like I was dead,' she said, frowning.

'What do you mean?' I studied the way she clenched her jaw, as if she was sucking on something bitter. 'It's hard to explain,' she replied.

A bird came by the window and peered into the kitchen. The birds seemed different here—scrawnier—perhaps because they didn't have as much to eat. 'You want to see my sprouts?' asked Suzanna, getting up. She went out the kitchen door and it creaked shut. For a split second, I thought she was gone again and that she might not come back. There was only silence. There was only the hum of the fan. Then the door creaked open and Suzanna swept in, bearing a tray of seeds. She spoke about mung beans, coriander, mint and thyme, pointing to this tray and that in that graceful way of hers.

She glowed like Pa, displaying the same luminance he sometimes had. And I thought it was true that people who look alike tend to be attracted to each other. Cupping her mug, she asked, 'How is your father?' I saw her eyes go soft and I wondered if she still had any feelings for him.

'Ah Ma died,' I replied.

'I heard.' Suzanna frowned, as if she herself was in pain.

'Why didn't you go to the funeral?'

Suzanna shifted in her seat. 'I couldn't.' I was not sure if she meant 'couldn't' or 'didn't' or 'wasn't allowed to'. She gazed out of the window, silent again.

'I saw Lily there,' I said. 'She gave me this.' I handed Suzanna the photo.

When she looked at it, her face lit up. 'My dress!' she exclaimed, covering her smile with her hand. She seemed to have this ability to switch expressions within a second—old, young, happy, sad. As she studied the picture, I saw the piano in the corner. It was a Petrof, like the one we had in Melbourne.

'Do you still play?' I gestured towards it.

She shook her head. And so, this was how it was. Question, answer, question, answer, until she looked at her watch and said she had to go out soon. She placed her grey scarf back over her head, twisting the ends swiftly and elegantly. It reminded me of Dessi's Aunt Katarina, who could apply lipstick without looking at a mirror.

I put down my cup and asked about the toilet.

'Over there,' she said, gesturing towards a corridor. I walked down to the last room and grasped the door handle.

'No!' she yelled. Her voice rattled the walls of the house. 'No,' she said, a little more softly. 'The first door, on the left.'

* * *

When I came out, Suzanna was all dressed up. Scarf over her head, clipped just beneath the jaw. Bag slung over her shoulder. As she folded a dishcloth, we heard a commotion outside. A crowd had gathered in front of a building, a community hall perhaps. There were green flags fluttering near the entrance. All the women there had headscarves on, and the men were a sea of black heads.

'Are you ready to go?' said Suzanna.

'What's going on out there?'

'I'm not sure. Where's your bag?'

There was a woman on stage wearing a loose grey gown. A
man stood behind her, holding some kind of staff. It looked like a
play in the Botanical Gardens—*Hamlet* or *King Lear*. Everyone was
watching as she just stood there, her head bent down. It could not
be real. The man raised his arm. The cane came hurtling down on
the lady's back with a sound so loud I thought her bones cracked,
but it must have been her voice, or the gasp of the crowd. Three,
four, five times, a cry with each stroke.

'What's going on, what did she do?' I asked. Was this a show?
What was happening? Suzanna adjusted her scarf calmly and said
I should go. Another man stepped onto the stage, holding a loud
hailer. You could hear his voice echoing from all corners of the
village. He stood in his shiny Malay outfit, casting a spell over the
sea of people. The only words I could understand were Malaysia
this and Malaysia that, the rest was a blur of Malay.

In the end, he shouted, '*Hidup Melayu*! Hidup Melayu!' and
everyone cheered.

'What does that mean?' I said.

'Long live the Malays,' said Suzanna. There was an emotionless
quality to her voice as it echoed through the room. 'Sorry, I need
to go.' She glanced at the clock on the wall. 'We can talk more
next time.'

Suzanna watched as I gathered my things. Her eyes flitted
from the sofa to the trees outside, and back to the sofa. 'You got
everything?' she said.

'Yeah.' I hitched my bag over my shoulder and asked, 'When
can I see you again?'

Her mouth opened and closed. 'I'm not sure. I'll let you
know.' She pushed open the door grille and steered me towards
the verandah. She peered at the road, shielding her eyes from the
sun, and then she froze. I could see it. Her whole body went stiff.
A man opened the front gate, his shirt glistening in the sun. He
was like a ball of light drifting towards us. '*Assailamualaikum*,' he

called out. Suzanna replied in kind. Up close, he wasn't very tall, about Suzanna's height. But he exuded the same charisma and confidence he had used to control the crowd.

I was not sure how to behave or what to expect. The man beating the girl was bad but this guy standing in front of me pierced me with an even deeper chill. Perhaps it was the way he looked at Suzanna, saying nothing. Or the way she seemed to shrink into herself. He looked at me with searing eyes. 'Katie,' said Suzanna. 'This is Tun Said.'

Chapter 14

Yellow Mission

The next day was a Saturday, so Roy and Maggie were around. During the week, Roy went to some college in Subang Jaya and Maggie went to a girls' school in the city. Roy was doing the equivalent of Year 12 and Maggie was in Year 10. After school, there were things like football, netball, Maths tuition and art class, so I hardly saw them much except for the evenings.

Saturdays, it turns out, were pretty chill. At 9 a.m., neither of them had come downstairs. At about 10 a.m., Maggie trudged down. She stifled a yawn but was already dressed in a stylishly baggy T-shirt and shorts, her lips sparkling with a pearly pink lipstick. When she saw me reading in the living room, she smiled and asked if I wanted to follow them out.

'Sure,' I said. Pa was busy with the lawyers again. And if it was anything like the last few days, he would only finish late in the evening. Roy made an appearance about an hour later, hair still wet from a shower. After he'd had a quick bite, the three of us jumped into his white Charade and sped towards the neighbourhood town centre. I thought it would be Pete's Place again, but Roy drove past the turn.

'Where are we going?' I asked. Maggie exchanged glances with Roy. 'Just down there,' she said, pointing vaguely towards the traffic light. Roy made a left turn, and after a few more swerves, stopped at the end of a cul-de-sac. I got out of the car and saw the golden arches of McDonald's in the distance, where Pete's Place was. So, we were not far at all, just in the midst of a nearby housing area.

'Over here,' Roy waved from a rusty gate.

'Wait,' I said, pointing at a 'No Trespassers' sign—or at least that's what I thought it said. The words were in Malay but there was a graphic of a man pointing a rifle at another man. 'It's okay,' Roy said, beckoning me to follow.

Stones crunched under our feet as we trudged towards a courtyard that had an enormous tree sprouting out from the centre. 'What is this place?' I asked.

'It used to be a school,' Roy replied.

The tree looked like part of the building, growing between two blocks. Its branches reached up into the sky and tiny swallows darted between its crevices. I followed Roy and Maggie up a flight of stairs and stopped in front of a door the colour of peaches. Roy knocked—two long knocks, followed by three short ones. The door opened. A boy with a long fringe stylishly backcombed, peeked out. When I saw the gold chain glinting around his neck, I recognized him as Shang, the singer of Roy's band.

All the windows slats were shut, except for a broken pane which let in a rectangle of light. I clutched the strap of my bag as we approached the bunch of people sitting around a table at the far end of the room. Everyone stopped what they were doing. 'Who's she?' a girl sneered. She had short boyish hair and wore a pair of New Balance runners; the kind of girl who probably wore jeans and runners everywhere. Roy introduced her as Jane and me as his cousin from Australia. 'So Katie's going to be helping us,' explained Roy.

I shot Maggie a look. She just smiled back.

'Really?' Jane said. 'Does she even know what Mentari is?'

'Oh, is this for a Mentari rally?' I said. I took in the reams of yellow paper on the table. 'I know about it!' Pa had shown us pictures on the Malaysia Kini website. They called it the Malaysian Spring, alluding to the fields of yellow 'flowers' suddenly cropping up all over the city. No one knew who was doing it but first one suburb had it, then another and another. Yellow was the colour of the Mentari group, who were rallying for fair and clean elections, so the 'flowers' were a call for justice, for the birth of a new and fairer Malaysia. 'You guys are the ones that have been doing the flags?'

'Not all of them,' Jane said, sniffing somewhat proudly. 'There are a few different groups.' She tabulated my presence through her big square glasses, then made space for me at the table. She introduced me to a few others there—Mike, Mei, Chen, Jude—I forgot their names soon after, but they smiled and nodded warmly. Soon, I joined them in cutting, folding and sticking, to the sounds of some Indie music playing in the background.

Throughout this time, Shang eyed us from across the room. He wasn't doing any flag-making but was engrossed in something on his laptop. As I placed my third flag down, a Chinese boy slid into the seat beside me. He had the purest white skin and eyes that stretched charmingly into slits when he smiled. 'Hey,' he chirped. 'I'm Leong.'

'I'm Katie,' I said. I told him I liked his bracelet, pointing to the twisted threads around his wrist. He laughed and said it was from the temple. 'It's for prayers,' he explained. 'The monk gives it for blessings.'

'Oh,' I replied, blushing. Leong continued to smile, unperturbed. He started asking me all sorts of questions about Australia—whether I'd been to the Big Day Out, or seen Powder Finger and other bands I'd never heard of.

'What's with the accent?' said Roy from across the table. 'She's from Melbourne, not Liverpool.' Everyone laughed.

I busied myself with sticking a piece of yellow paper onto a stick. A sense of excitement thrummed in my chest as chatter rose around the table. They spoke about the racial tension growing in the country and how things had changed.

'I don't know how things got so Islamic,' said Mei. 'During my parents' time, they used to have friends of all backgrounds come over and drink. Now things are so awkward.'

'I know what you mean,' said Jane. 'Now they're telling us to get out of the country. My ancestors have been here since the nineteenth century. They worked in the tin mines, they built houses and factories; I mean, they practically built this city. Then this guy comes up and says, "you don't belong here, go back to your own country".'

I nodded quietly. Every country had the same issues, didn't it? I thought of that guy yelling at Pa outside Dan Murphy's, telling him to go back to his own country. 'The thing is,' went on Jane. 'They believe him.'

'Who?' I asked.

'The rural Malays,' she explained. 'They really think it's their country and everything he says is true.'

'Yeah,' chimed in Maggie. 'The other day, he had this rally at an Islamic high school, telling the kids they had to fight for their country; he said they needed to take their land back. What, is he trying to start a war?'

'Who is this guy?' I asked.

'Tun Said, have you heard of him?'

My hand froze in mid-air. 'Yeah, he's in the news a lot, isn't he?'

My throat was dry. My heart pounded as I slowly placed my flag down and picked up another. When I finished cutting the paper, Roy tapped me on the shoulder. 'Got a minute?'

* * *

We walked down the stairs and ambled down the corridor. Dried leaves rustled in the drain beside us. 'Leong's nice,' I said.

'Yeah,' said Roy, striding beside me in a pair of white Adidas sneakers. Even at his leisurely pace, it was a slight effort for me to keep up. 'He was at Pete's Place.'

'He was?'

'Yeah, he played bass.'

'Oh, yeah,' I said, recalling a small guy dressed in black.

Roy continued walking, a slight frown on his forehead. When we reached a grassy space at the back of the building, he stopped. I heard birds chirping from the bushes. *Kurik . . . kurik*, they sang. *Kurik . . . kurik*. I peered through the branches. What colour were they—green or brown, or rainbow like the parakeets in our garden?

Roy gripped the 100 Plus bottle in his hand and it let out a small groan. He glanced at me, then back at the ground where tiny pink puff balls sat in the grass. Finally, he looked up again. 'Were you with Justin Reza yesterday?'

'Who?'

Roy frowned as if he was struggling with his words. 'Shang said he saw you at Kampung Damai yesterday . . .' 'Oh . . .' He was talking about Justin. Had he seen me with Suzanna too?

'You're not supposed to go there,' said Roy.

'Why?'

'It's a Wira area, we don't go there. Remember I told you this before?' Roy looked at me evenly as if trying to see inside my head.

'I was looking for my mum,' I said. 'Did you know she was alive? Did you know she was here?' My voice grew louder with every word and I met Roy's gaze.

He stared back at me as if contemplating an equation. Then he pressed his lips together. 'I only found out a few years ago. My mum mentioned she was back but we never really spoke to her.'

A weight slammed down on my chest. 'Why?' I said.

'She's not allowed to come to the house. Whenever she came over, mum told us to stay in our rooms.'

'Why?'

Roy scratched the back of his ear. 'They said she could charm people.'

'What?'

'Charm—like cast a spell. My mum said that's what she did to your dad.'

'Really?'

Kurik-kurik, kurik-kurik. The chorus of birds began to chirp louder.

'I don't know,' Roy said. 'All I know is that they were pretty brave to be together.'

'What do you mean?' Roy took a deep breath and scanned the tips of the trees. Then he turned back to me. 'Don't you know why your parents left?'

* * *

When I was old enough to wonder, I asked Pa why we were in Melbourne and he said, 'For a better life'. He said it in a way that didn't matter; like it was something people did all the time, like going to the shops or going for swimming lessons.

On that little grassy bank that day, Roy told me about my mum and dad.

'If you marry a Muslim here, you have to convert,' he explained. 'So your dad converted on paper, but he didn't really follow it. I mean they celebrated Hari Raya but he still went to church and sometimes your mum even followed him, it was all pretty relaxed. But when the riots happened, your parents were one of the first people targeted.'

'What riots?'

Roy gave me a look that said I really didn't know anything about my country. 'The May Riots,' he said. He told me how the Malays were fighting the Chinese and the Chinese were fighting the Malays. Pa and Suzanna came over one evening with me in tow. Someone had thrown stones at Suzanna and tried to set Pa's car on fire. It wasn't safe for them anymore.

'Who did that?'

'Some people from the Wira group. They started acting like the police, hunting down people who didn't follow Muslim rules and beating you up if they thought you were doing something wrong.'

'Were they allowed to do that?'

'They just did it.' Roy shrugged. 'A lot of non-Malays left the country then. They didn't feel safe anymore.'

I thought of what Jane and Maggie had spoken about in the classroom. 'Are things better now?'

Roy frowned. 'They got better after a while, as in no more riots happened. But recently . . .'

'Recently what?'

'The Wira group has gotten more popular, I'm not sure why. They've actually got some political power now and it's growing. Most of them live in Kampung Damai. That's where they meet; that's where they have their rallies. That's why none of us go there.'

I could feel the hardness of a rock underneath my shoe. 'My mother is there,' I said in quiet voice.

'She's not who you think she is.'

'I don't think anything, I don't even know her.' The wind blew and I could smell the heat off the long grass. 'How do you know she is with them?' I said.

'They are all with them. Haven't you heard what they do?'

I recalled the man on stage bringing down the whip on the young girl. The bushes in front of us shook. Two large birds stepped out. They were neither sweet nor pretty, just big and black.

* * *

Later that evening, Roy and I were scampering down a hill in Lake Gardens. We stopped halfway to admire the yellow flags we had just planted. The slope bloomed like a sea of flowers; the city lights twinkled in the background.

'Looks good,' Roy said.

'Yeah,' I said, a quiet joy swelling in my chest.

Roy looked at me. 'So will you stop going to the village?'

'What?'

'Kampung Damai, you'll stop going there?'

My heart thumped.

'The only reason Shang let you come with us is because I told him you were on our side and that you would stop going there.'

Roy's eyes were fixed on me, asking me to understand. I said nothing. The grass quivered around us. Roy looked at me for a moment longer then he continued making his way downwards. I followed, the gravel crunching loudly beneath my feet.

Chapter 15

Breakfast

After seeing Suzanna, I still hadn't had the chance to talk to Pa about it. He always seemed busy with Ah Ma's estate stuff. So when I saw him sitting in the kitchen the next morning, I knew this was the time.

'Morning,' I said.

'Hey.' He stirred a mug with dainty English roses on it.

'Did you get back late last night?' I asked in a light voice.

'Sorry, were you waiting up?'

'No, not really.' I casually picked up a glass. 'You going out again today?'

'Mm-hm.'

'Where were you last night?'

'I had a meeting.'

'With the lawyers?'

'No . . . just some work stuff.' Pa brushed the top of his nose. 'I didn't know you still have work here . . .'

'I still have a few things going on. Hey, do you want some Milo? I'll make you some.'

Before I could answer, Pa went over to the pantry and took out a can of Milo. He made it his usual way—three table spoons of powder, lots of condensed milk. When he placed it in front of me, I said, 'Do you want to meet for lunch? I can meet you somewhere.'

'Maybe not.' He glanced at his watch. 'I'll be running around here and there.' Pa reached out for a tea towel with the words 'Australia' on it. The clock on the wall ticked. Tick. Tick. It resonated all around as he shoved some files into a bag. 'I saw Mum yesterday,' I blurted.

'What?' said Pa, lowering his bag.

'Why didn't you tell me she was alive?' I said. 'Why did she leave?' I could feel a heat simmering in my chest. It kept bubbling up and I kept trying to keep it down.

'Were you ever going to tell me?' My voice sounded strangled.

Pa frowned. He gritted his teeth and put his bag on the chair. 'Sorry,' he said. 'I didn't think you would ever see her again.'

I gawked at him. It was the kind of sorry you said when you bumped into someone on the bus or stepped on a dog's tail. Pa fiddled with the strap of his bag. He placed it on the shoulder of the chair but it slipped off again. After he put it back on, he said, 'How did you see her anyway?' Did she come here?'

I told Pa about Lily at the funeral. I told him about Kampung Damai and the beautiful house among the trees. The more I spoke, the stiffer his jaw became. 'You need to stop going there,' he said.

'Why? Give me a good reason.'

'The people there are different,' he explained. 'They live in a different kind of world.'

Why is she there then? If they are bad people, why is she there?

Pa glanced at his phone. 'I'm sorry,' he said. 'I need to go.'

What could be more important than this? It's not like I had asked him to help me with some homework or discuss a TV show. It was always like this, me asking Pa something and him slinking off somewhere and forgetting about it, too wrapped up in whatever he seemed to be wrestling with in his head. 'We'll talk this evening, okay?' he said. 'I'll try to get back early.'

Pa's hair was slicked to the side, his trousers were neatly pressed. He looked like someone from a magazine; someone I didn't know. He slung his satchel over his shoulder and then he left. The front door let out a small creak and then it slammed shut, leaving me in the silence of the house.

Chapter 16

Newtown

Funny that Pa was so insistent about me not going to Kampung Damai. He was usually chill about a lot of things. In Year 5, I was taking the bus to school. Over here in KL, he was happy to let me wander around the malls. I recalled Roy's troubled expression that day at the Lake Gardens as if I was committing a crime by saying I couldn't stop going to the village; as if I was breaking some sacred fraternity I had newly become a part of. So instead of replying to Suzanna's messages or dialling for a cab, I opened up my English textbook and began reading about a certain Edward Kelly, otherwise known as Ned Kelly.

Later that afternoon, when I had resumed my assignment, Maggie strode into my room. She picked up my Ned Kelly book and scrutinized the guy with the metal helmet. 'Is that The Wizard of Oz?'

'No, that's Ned Kelly . . . a bushranger,' I added. She continued to frown. I explained that he was a famous outlaw in the nineteenth century, who stole horses and shot at whoever he thought was wrong. Some people thought he was a hero of the ordinary people who fought against the police and stood up for people who were wrongly accused.

A bit like a Mentari leader, actually! Maybe I should include that in my essay—the similarities between Malaysian opposition groups and the Australian bushranger movement. Before I could tell Maggie about this, she had already moved on to my chest of drawers. 'What's this?' She held up my thermometer. 'Are you sick?'

'No.'

She gave me a funny look and put the thermometer back. 'Do you want to come out with us to eat?'

'Oh, yes. Whereabouts this time?' I recalled the incredible roast duck we'd had the other night, slippery noodles, under a bridge, eaten in the glow of street lights. Then there was that Indian curry house, where you used a banana leaf as a plate and waiters doused your rice in a range of glorious curries. I wondered where our next culinary adventure would be. 'Newtown,' Maggie replied.

'What kind of food do they have?'

'All kinds, it's a food court.'

* * *

'Food court' was an understatement. When I got out of Roy's car, he pointed at a building across the road. The first floor was ablaze with stalls which stretched all the way from one end of the street to the other. Roy was already starting to walk ahead, about to step into the path of a car. 'What are you doing?' I yelled.

'Crossing,' he replied. He stepped back from the path of the car—a Honda—that did not end up stopping. It wheezed past us so closely, I could feel the heat from its door.

'Isn't there a pedestrian crossing?' I said.

'What do you mean?'

'Like a light where we can cross?'

'No.' Roy frowned as if I was the one who was insane. He took another step forward, squinting at the oncoming headlights. 'Come on,' he said. 'If you don't move, they will never let us go.' He stuck out his hand and the car heading towards us slowed down. It seemed totally unnatural, like jumping off a cliff or

breathing underwater, but I followed him and Maggie across the
road. This time, the cars did slow down, slamming down their
brakes as they approached, daring us to cross. The trick was to
not hesitate. 'Just keep walking,' said Roy as a car pulled to a halt
inches before my knees.

When we reached the other side, we found ourselves in the
midst of the night market crowd. We followed the thick swarm of
people as they hovered over different stalls, each one more bizarre
than the next. Tables of CDs spread out like an assortment of
lollies—Radiohead, S Club 7, Black Eyed Peas. Hello Kitty socks,
shiny clips. I was examining a claw clip when a jackhammer
boomed right next to my elbow. I turned around and saw a man
grinding a boulder of ice in a large machine. He turned the ice
shavings into a mountain of snow and drizzled it with pink rose
syrup. When I looked up, I saw Maggie and Roy ascending a broad
staircase. I ran after them, tackling the steps two at a time until
I reached the bright lights of Newtown.

It was about 7.21 p.m. and office workers were streaming in
for dinner alongside students like us. The Barbie girl song blared
from one of the market stalls below. It felt like a nightclub of
gastronomical delights. Everywhere I turned, there was food
sizzling, smoking, simmering, gleaming; golden curry flecks as
dazzling as the night. 'We usually go over there,' Maggie yelled,
pointing to my right. I spotted Leong and Shang sitting in front
of a Taiwanese dessert stall. We joined them.

Everyone went to order different things. Shang got Indomie
goreng from the mamak stall. Leong got a black pepper steak.
Roy got a Ramli burger. Before long, all these different plates of
food arrived. Mine was the last to come—Yong Tau Fu, or okra
stuffed with fish paste served with rice noodles in a clear chicken
broth, similar to what I'd had on the first day at Tua Ee's house.
I whipped the wooden chopsticks out of the plastic bag they
came in and began wiping my spoon with a tissue. I wiped every
inch of it, including the handle. I knew what the workers did—I'd

seen them wash cutlery in the back alleys; the tubs of soapy black water and rats scurrying in the drains.

There I was, another dark-haired patron among a sea of black heads. From a drone's view, I'd look like anyone there: black hair, T-shirt, slurping up soup or taking a swig from a glass. And yet, I didn't quite feel like anyone there. A strange sound hummed around me. Office workers roared with laughter, lanyards shaking against their pin-striped shirts. To my right, a Chinese family chomped on chilli pipis and boiled squid. I listened to Maggie speak to her friend in a sing-song voice. 'Is that Mandarin?' I asked.

'No, Cantonese.'

'How many languages can you speak?'

Maggie thought for a second. 'Mandarin, English, Malay, Cantonese—four.' She paused. 'Five, if you include Hokkien.' She was really nonchalant about it. I felt completely inadequate knowing how to speak only one language. I wished I was smarter, better, cooler. The rice noodles slipped off my chopstick and disappeared into the soup.

Leong came back to the table like he'd won the lottery. 'Guess what, guys? Uncle Wong has Musang King! Who wants some?' A chorus of 'Me!' rang around the table.

'What is Musang King?' I whispered to Maggie.

'It's a type of durian,' she replied.

Not long after, Leong returned with two styrofoam boxes. The moment he opened them, the smell of rotten eggs ripped through the air. All around the table, Maggie and the others swooned over the fruit as if it was the most delicious thing on earth. 'Oh my god, look at this one, it looks so good.' Maggie bit into the shiny yellow flesh and a thick cream oozed out.

I took a photo of the other box—still intact—and sent it to Dessi.

Me   : Guess what this is?

'Katie, you haven't had any,' pointed out Roy.

'It's okay,' I replied. 'I don't really want any.'

Everyone gasped as if I was saying no to the elixir of life itself.

'Have you had durian before?' Roy asked.

'Not really.'

'Try some, it tastes better than it looks.'

'You can't come to Malaysia and not have durian,' added Leong.

'Take this one.' Maggie offered the box to me with two hands.

'Okay,' I said tentatively. The whole fruit was wrapped in some kind of translucent skin that glistened under the stall lights. I took a small bite . . .

'Do you like it?' asked Maggie.

The explosion of flavours in my mouth made me gag. The first things that came to mind were smelly socks, a drain and baby poo. Everyone chuckled and Roy patted me on the shoulder. He motioned to the phone lighting up in my hand. 'Tell your friend how awesome it is.'

I smiled back weakly. It wasn't Dessi.

Suzanna   : How are you? Still busy with Tua Ee?

'Do you want some more?' said Roy.

'No thanks.' I slipped the phone into my bag. 'You can have mine.'

'No, I'm having it,' interjected Leong.

As Leong and Roy fought over the last few pieces, I thought about the messages Suzanna had sent me throughout the day. I had not replied. Every time I tried, I thought of Roy or Shang or Pa. In the end, it was better to do nothing. Roy gave me a gentle pat on the shoulder. 'You okay?'

'Yes.' I smiled. I sipped on my lime juice as I felt the phone in my bag continue to glow like a piece of hot coal.

* * *

Suzanna had messaged early that morning. I said I was busy with Tua Ee. Then she messaged again, and again a few hours later. I just didn't know what to say. The laughter around me grew louder, combined with smoke from a satay stall. I found it harder and harder to breathe. 'Where's the toilet?' I asked Maggie.

'It's at the end of the block,' she said. 'Near Steven's Corner—the char kuey teow stall.'

And so, I made my way to the end of the block, where I saw a sign that said Steven's Corner. A man, presumably Steven, stood over the wok like the devil himself. He threw a handful of meat into the oil and flames leapt around his body. The sounds of sizzling pierced the air. I slipped past the crowd and followed the toilet signs pointing upstairs. As I went up flight after flight, the hum of the food court began to disappear.

The restrooms were a doorway of light. I went in, I came out. In the quiet of the corridor, in the dim glow, it was easier to breathe, away from the crowd and the smells and the messages waiting on my phone. I was about to head down when I saw the stairs continue to lead upwards. Maybe it was the breeze that night or the way the sky twinkled but I followed the steps up and found myself on the roof of the building. I walked to the edge and stared out at the Twin Towers glistening in the distance. The city was huge—a million lights blinked and twinkled back at me, highways zipped up and down in all directions. I felt like the tiniest speck in the universe.

'Hey,' a voice said.

My heart lurched in fear as I whipped my head around. Through the twilight, I made out the hazy shape of Justin. 'Yikes,' I said. 'You scared me.' An amber bud glowed from his fingers. 'You smoke?' I said. He let out a stream of white. 'Don't you know it's bad for you? A cigarette has like seven thousand chemicals in it and seventy are linked to cancer.'

'Did you read that on the Internet?'

I glared at him. 'I'm just saying.' *Every time you smoke, you shorten your life by eleven seconds. Second-hand smoke kills too. People around you can get heart disease, brain tumours and lung cancer.* Of course, I didn't say this to him. I simply moved a few steps away.

Justin took a final puff and flicked away his cigarette. Then he came over and stood beside me. Surprisingly, he didn't smell toxic at all. Usually, I avoided anything and anyone that had to do with smoking, but for some reason I felt slightly drawn to it; the way a car passes a bus and feels sucked into its gravitational pull. The scent from Justin was gentle. Warm. Woody. For a moment, I even wondered what it would be like to kiss someone who smoked. *Oh my god, where did that come from?* Could the nicotine be affecting my brain already?

'Why do you smoke?' I asked.

'I just need to do something with my hands.'

'Can't you like, twirl a pencil?'

'It's not as fun.' Justin leaned against the railing then his face lit up. 'I can do origami.'

'Really?'

He felt around his pockets and pulled out a receipt. I recalled the meticulous way he had folded his chewing gum wrapper at the funeral. He did the same with the receipt.

Fold, unfold. Sharp tip, perfect crease. His fingers swivelled around so quickly, I could not follow his moves. After one final press, Justin held up a white crane before me.

'Thanks,' I said, admiring the bird in my palm. The gentle breeze made it tip to its side. 'Hey,' I said. 'What are you doing here anyway? Were you at Newtown too?'

'Yes, we're there a lot.'

'Really? Roy and Maggie go there a lot too. Where are you sitting?'

'Near the Taiwanese dessert place. You?'

'Near the Thai Tom Yam shop.'

'Oh, on the other end.'

Justin took out some chewing gum from his pocket and offered me a stick. When I declined, he popped it into his mouth. 'Why are you up here, anyway?' I asked.

Justin shrugged. 'I like the view.'

'The Twin Towers?'

'No, just everything.' He pointed to the street below. Umbrellas bloomed along the road, selling the greatest assortment of items: socks, peanut pancakes, orchids, Siamese fighting fish glowering in square bowls. 'I like the vibe of the market,' he explained. 'There's a good energy about it.'

I guess I knew what he meant. Across the road, somebody guffawed and the noise that rose from the crowd was almost melodious, a bit like the sea. Amidst this hum, the trill of a piano cut through the night and for a moment, it was all I could hear. It was a song I'd heard a million times before, ringing through the hallway of our house or bumbling against the walls of my bedroom. Now it soared over this world I didn't really know— rusty railings, a clothesline, patches of black on concrete.

'Max Benez.' Justin said.

'You know it?' I whispered.

'Yeah, I like a lot of old stuff like Neil Young, The Byrds . . . I'm surprised *you* know it.'

'He was my mother's favourite singer.'

'I see.'

The thought of Suzanna made me quiet. As if on cue, the phone in my bag buzzed and I gripped the strap of my bag.

'What's wrong?' asked Justin.

'Nothing.' I frowned. I clutched the hard rectangle of my phone in my bag and asked him, 'Have you ever done something that everyone says you shouldn't do?'

'Yeah, all the time!' Justin's eyes shone.

'No, I'm serious.'

Justin stared out at the buildings and I recalled how his shirt had gleamed at the mosque. 'Hey,' I said. 'You live in Kampung Damai, right?'

'Yeah.'

'What's it like living there?'

'What do you mean?'

'You're with the Wira group, right?'

'No.' There was a hardness to Justin's voice, his eyes grew dark.

'Isn't everyone there?'

'Of course not! Just because I live there, doesn't mean I'm with them. They're just this group. I have nothing to do with them.'

'Why are you being so sensitive?'

'I'm not.' Justin scowled.

'I see, I just got the impression that everyone there was—'

'No,' he said, cutting me off. 'They're not.'

Justin frowned even more and I wondered if I had said something wrong. At the same time, I felt a small window of hope open. Maybe I just needed to talk to Suzanna. Maybe she wasn't really with Wira. 'I need to go,' I announced.

'Are you angry? I just didn't like the way you assumed that—'

'No, no, I'm not angry. Thank you,' I said.

'For what?'

'For the chat.'

Justin's frown slipped away. He tilted his head and some curls fell over his jaw. Then he smiled. 'You're welcome.'

Chapter 17

Tea

When I reached Suzanna's house, it smelt like a pinewood forest. Not from the garden but from the windows. The scent seeped into the air and became stronger when she opened the door. 'You're here!' She beamed. 'For a moment, I was worried you were ignoring me but I guess you must be busy. Come in, come in.' She put the kettle on the stove and the flame underneath sprang to life. 'Have you had spruce tea before? It's good for clearing the mind.'

She bustled about, taking out two cups from the cupboard, moving here and there, from the kitchen table to the sink, throwing out scraps and wiping plates as if I came over for tea all the time; as if there was no nine-year chasm between our lives.

'Why did you leave?' I asked. My voice was loud and clear in the quiet room.

'What?'

'Why did you leave Melbourne?'

I watched Suzanna grip the dishcloth in her hand. I did not take my eyes off her, did not give her any opportunity to look elsewhere. 'My father was sick,' she said softly. 'He needed me here.'

'As in, why didn't you come back?'

Suzanna's eyes scanned the room, then flitted back to the kitchen table. I braced myself for the answer. Inside, I kind of knew. I thought of that day in the kitchen when I'd come in from playing in the garden. Suzanna—Mum—had just thrown all the groceries onto the floor. I still remembered the cornflakes and oranges all over the tiles. 'I can't do this anymore,' she said. 'I'm tired. I'm so tired of it.'

As Pa tried to console her, I remembered my favourite blue bowl with the puppy face overturned in the corner, the puppy face with its happy tongue oblivious to the tension in the room, and I knew it was about me. I always thought that was what killed her—this tiredness, this burden she had to bear as a parent. But there she stood in front of me, alive, and I knew now that the burden had not killed her—it had simply driven her away.

Suzanna frowned and contemplated the cup in hand. 'It's hard to explain,' she said in a faltering voice. 'Have you ever felt like you just had to get away from everything?'

'Was it that bad?' I winced.

'I just felt like I didn't belong there,' she explained. 'I came back because my father was sick. But the longer I stayed, the more I felt like it wasn't right to go back.'

Suzanna bit her lip. 'I felt like I belonged here.' Suzanna said she had missed Melbourne a little when she was here, but when she was in Melbourne, she missed Malaysia more. She said Melbourne was quiet, too quiet. She had missed the nightlife in Malaysia, the food, the people.

'So you were homesick . . .' I said.

'Yes, but it was not just that.' She scanned the room. 'Can you hear that?'

'What?'

'You know that sound you hear when you stop to listen to a place? Like a buzz.'

I pricked up my ears. 'The children? The cars?'

'All of it.' She told me it was the voices, the market, the chink of a spatula on a wok. All I could hear was the pot bubbling on the stove.

* * *

We spoke for a few minutes more, or more like I watched her speak; her expressions changed from happy to thoughtful to wistful. It was only when she put her cup down that the words began to become clear again.

'I knew it wouldn't be fair on you to have you come back here,' she said. 'I wanted you to have a better life.'

'A better life.' I repeated her words as if I was turning them slowly in my mouth.

'Wasn't it?' she asked.

I clutched the strap of my bag and thought of all those times I had cried myself to sleep, spending days huddled up in bed. Would it not have been better to know she was somewhere out there in the great beyond, even if she wasn't there with me? 'I don't understand why you guys had to lie about it.'

Suzanna nodded like she understood, like everything I said was valid and right. 'I just wanted to disappear,' she said. 'I felt like I wasn't fit to be your mum and it was better if I was gone. Maybe it was a mistake—'

'I was a mistake?'

'No, not you. The whole situation. I . . .'

'You just got tired.'

'Yes.' Suzanna's gaze snapped up. Despite the smooth, shiny skin, I noticed the bags under her eyes, as if she too had spent nights tossing and turning, or blinking into the night. She looked relieved, and then afraid. A deep resentment began to grow in my chest. 'I know you're angry,' she said. 'And I don't expect you to forgive me but you know what, seeing you that day in front of my house . . . It was like—'

I stood up. The wind squeezed through the cracks in the house. Everything told me to flee, to stay far away from all these lies and get back to my life. I was about to spin around to leave when Suzanna said, 'Do you know why I named you Katherine?'

'No.'

'Your dad and I went to Egypt for our honeymoon and there was a monastery there called St Katherine's. It was the most beautiful building I'd ever seen.'

'Why are you telling me this?'

'I just wanted you to know . . .'

'That book.' She pointed to a leatherbound book on the shelf, a golden tab peeking out. 'That was your grandfather's. He was a famous *imam*, you know, someone who leads prayers in a mosque.'

I observed the book, the photos of a man in a long white gown. Suzanna began telling me things about random things from around the room, as if gifting me some last pieces of knowledge. Beneath the books in the bottom-most shelf were the Britannica encyclopaedia—the entire collection from A to Z. She and her father used to pore over them for hours in the days before Internet and phones—when you couldn't just pluck knowledge out of the sky. 'I know most of it is outdated now, but I couldn't bring myself to get rid of it.'

Suzanna showed me photos and newspaper cuttings, a bowl her father had used to pound leaves into powder. Soon, I developed this hazy image of my grandparents on holiday in Egypt, riding camels across the desert; young Suzanna listening to her father, fascinated by his stories about the herbs and plants in his garden.

All these scenes swept around me until my gaze rested on a basket of the most peculiar vegetables. They had large bulbous roots, the soil still clinging to its tendrils. 'What is that?' I asked.

'Burdock,' she replied. 'I just harvested it from the garden.'

The aroma of wood floated out from the basket, this leafy smell that reminded me of a forest. 'You can use it to make soup and the stems can be eaten. I was thinking of making a tea for detoxing. But it takes a while; you have to strip the outer layer bit by bit, and then slice it up into thin pieces.' Suzanna studied my face. 'Do you . . . want to help?'

I'm not sure if it was because I wanted to stay or because I had nowhere else to go, but I took off my bag and went back to the table.

Chapter 18

The Visitor

The next day, Roy and Maggie asked if I wanted to join them for another flag-making session. They called it helping them with a 'project'. I said no, I had to catch up on some schoolwork, which they promptly believed. (Maggie had told Roy about my logbook habit.) After they left, I made my way to Suzanna's house again.

There was something different about the air that day. A green Mercedes was parked by the side of the road, a Twisties wrapper fluttered near its tyre. When I pushed the gate open, a flock of sparrows scattered. I couldn't shake off the feeling that I was forgetting something.

Suzanna's house was always full of scents, depending on what she was brewing that day. You could catch the first hints from the driveway. One day, it would smell like a forest. The next day, it would be citrusy. Today, it was something sweet, like honeysuckle. But it wasn't the smell that stopped me. It was the voices.

I went round to the side of the house and hid behind a pot of heliconias. Through the long red buds of dynamite, I saw Suzanna sitting on a sofa. A man sat on the armchair, his back towards me. Was it Tun Said? No. This man was taller, broader. He wore a blue button-down shirt and his hair was carefully slicked to the side the way it had been this morning on his way out to see the lawyers.

Pa stood up and went over to sit beside Suzanna. Suddenly, it all made sense. That was Tua Teow's old green Mercedes in the front; the one Pa had been using to get around. Was he looking for me? Was he angry?

'You need to stop coming here,' Suzanna said. 'He could come any time.'

'He won't.'

Then Pa did something I will never forget. He slid his arm around Suzanna in a way that seemed to swallow her up. The term 'embrace' popped into my head and I suddenly fathomed the enormity of the word. How often had he been coming here?

Pa gently released Suzanna and looked into her eyes. 'Did you tell her about . . .'

'Of course not,' replied Suzanna. 'We just chat about stuff. I . . .' The rest of her sentence was swallowed up by a mosque announcement. *Were they talking about me? What did she not tell me?* They continued to speak in soft tones like two people in a silent movie. Suzanna's brow was creased and furrowed. Every now and then, Pa would nod. The whole scene felt odd. It was as if I was the parent seeing my child with someone. Someone I did not know. I could not quite see her as a friend, much less my mother. How many times had Pa come here? All those times he had said he was going to the lawyers, had he been coming here?

Something brushed against my leg. It was the cat. It slunk between my calves with a loud meow. Pa and Suzanna did not seem to notice. A loud noise clattered on my right. I saw a jar spinning on the floor and the cat slinking away. This time, Pa and Suzanna looked up.

I ran out through the front gate and dashed into the bushes. I followed this trail and that trail, anything that would keep me off the main road, until I found myself in a different part of the village. The wind picked at my hair. I did not know which way to go. Each direction had the same long grass and clumps of ferns— then I heard the music. The notes trickled like fingers tugging me towards a grove of trees.

Chapter 19

The Shed

The music was coming from a building that looked like a cathedral. It had a high triangular roof and a wooden verandah in front. I crept up the steps and peeped through a window pane thick with dust. Two guys sat inside—one on a guitar, the other on drums. They were hunched over their instruments, jamming away.

The board under my foot creaked. Bright-green moss grew between the railings of the balcony. The air was quiet. Too quiet. I started to inch my way across the deck when the door flew open. A guy with deep brown skin scowled at me, his hair spiked up above his head. 'What are you doing?' he snarled. His gaze flicked to the trees, then back to my face.

'Hey, I know her,' said a voice from inside. Justin pushed the guy aside. 'What are you doing here?'

'I . . . I got a bit lost,' I stuttered.

'Okay.' He narrowed his eyes at me. 'Do you want to come inside?'

When Justin opened the door wider, I saw the other guy lower a metal pipe in his hand. Justin introduced me to him as Nasa. Standing there with the light on his face, he no longer looked threatening—more puppy than panther.

There was a big open space inside with some couches and chairs in the middle. The girl in the armchair was Tina.

I recognized her immediately as the girl from Pete's Place. She was wearing a long silver chain around her neck, the kind all the girls in school were wearing. She smiled at me and motioned to the couch. 'Where are you from?' she asked.

'What?'

'You're not Malaysian, right?'

'I'm from Australia,' I replied, flushing a little. 'I'm Roy's cousin. Roy is—'

'I know Roy.' Her voice was as smooth as honey. Everything about her was silky and smooth, from her black jeans and slinky black shirt to the sheen of her hair.

'How did you find us here?' she asked.

'I didn't. I mean not on purpose, I came from over there.' I gestured towards the trees.

'Oh, you came from the back.' she said. 'We thought you were the police.'

'The police? Why?'

'Not normal police, the Wira police.'

'Why? Are you not allowed to be here?'

'Probably not,' she said with a smirk.

'I see,' I said, looking around. 'What is this place anyway?'

Tina told me it was supposed to be a community hall but it was never completed. 'We call it The Shed,' she said.

I took in the buckets and spades in the corner. 'I guess it feels a bit like one.'

Tina continued to stare at me, a twinkle in her eye. 'Are you . . . mixed?'

'Mixed with what?'

'Your dad . . . is he Australian?'

'Oh no, he's Chinese.'

'And your mum?'

'Er . . . she's from here too.'

Tina tilted her head to one side. 'You should come by my shop some time,' she said.

'What shop?'

'Top Shop at Mid Valley. I work there on the weekend. We have a really nice Kate Moss collection that would look great on you.'

'Oh, okay,' I replied. I was not really into fashion. Most of my clothes were from Target or Cotton On, occasionally Sports Girl.

The strum of a guitar rang out and I saw that Justin and Nasa had resumed playing. They both had very different playing styles. Nasa hammered away on the drums in an almost reckless fashion. Meanwhile, Justin pressed each chord as if he were making imprints on silk.

Tina turned back to the book in front of her, presumably a textbook. She grabbed a pencil and scribbled little notes in the margins of the page. The sun frittered over us through the dust of the windows. I felt a sense of lightness as if I were in a place suspended in time. The sofa beside me was littered with musical odds and ends—a guitar, a bass, maracas, tambourine, some kind of bongo. I picked up the guitar and began plucking the strings softly. I'm not sure how long I was doing that for, but soon, the square piece of sunlight by the table had shifted to my feet.

'That's nice.' Justin said, appearing by my side. 'Why didn't you play that at Pete's Place?'

I shrugged. He continued standing there. 'Play something else.'

I shook my head. It was like when someone asks you to say something in another language and you just can't think of anything. But because he was standing and waiting so patiently, I picked up the guitar again.

I tried to ignore Justin watching my fingers but it was almost impossible to do so. After the first two lines, I messed up. I sighed.

'That was cool,' said Justin. 'Was it that song you played at Pete's Place?'

'Yeah, you could tell?'

'Yes, but it sounded a bit different.'

I'd played the Concerto in G but I played it my way—slow in the places I wanted it to be and a little quicker when I felt like it.

'Go again,' he said. 'You have really good tone.'

I frowned, not sure whether to believe him. I couldn't believe he'd recognized what I was trying to do. So I started again and played the whole first movement and when I stopped, I realized I'd forgotten he was there. 'That was great.' His eyes shone like he was my biggest fan.

Suddenly, they turned serious. 'Hey,' he said. 'What did you say your friend's name was?'

'What friend?'

'The one that lives in Villa Kemboja.'

'Oh.' I'd told him I was visiting a friend that day. 'Suzanna,' I replied.

'Suzanna Samad?'

'Suzanna Chen . . . I think.'

Justin went over to talk to Nasa and they both started to dig through a box.

'Why?' I asked.

Neither boy replied. Nasa pulled out a plastic bag and after some more rummaging, he held up a CD. He passed it to Justin, who passed it to me. 'You're right,' I heard Nasa mumble. 'They do look alike.' I examined the cover and saw a black-and-white photo of a lady. The words 'Suzanna Samad' were scrawled across her body in a shiny font and the lady who sat there on a stool was unmistakably Suzanna. No headscarf, long hair tumbling down her back. She gazed up at a single spotlight, a soft smile on her face, as if breathing in the essence of the light that shone upon her.

'Do you know this song?' said Justin bending over his guitar. He started plucking the strings and singing a couple of bars. When he looked up, I shook my head. He played another song and then another, and that's when it clicked. He hadn't even started singing. He started plucking the strings and a jolt ran through my body.

He changed chords ever so carefully, as if a thread might break. Every time he moved up the frets, the guitar squeaked in the most gentle and beautiful way. The words he sang were in Malay, but for some reason they sounded familiar.

I asked him to sing the chorus again. I picked up my guitar and began fiddling around with some of the chords. We played it maybe a dozen times, each time braver and more confident than before. I didn't realize how engrossed I was until we both stopped playing at the same time.

'That was awesome, guys,' said Nasa. 'Look.' He skipped over and showed me a video on his phone. It was Justin and I playing the song, two guitarists facing each other. Just as we started the second line, the sun broke through the window, a ray of particles sprinkling down upon us.

Justin offered me a bottle of mineral water. 'Thank you,' I said, taking a swig.

'Does the water taste different here?' he asked.

'Actually,' I said with a smile. 'It does taste a bit different.' Then I frowned. 'Why? This is just water, right?' I scanned the ingredients, searching for anything toxic.

'Yes,' said Justin, smiling. 'It's just water.'

Regardless, I took out my tub of vitamins and popped one into my mouth. Justin took a sip from his bottle. 'So, how do you know Suzanna?'

The water in my mouth hardened into a ball. Who was she? What should I say? I swallowed slowly and turned to Justin. 'Remember how I said my mum passed away?'

* * *

When Justin and Nasa returned to their instruments, I checked my phone. My last conversation was with Dessi. I'd told her about finding Suzanna and she'd said she couldn't believe it. She asked me what Suzanna was like and I realized that I had not taken any photos of her. 'She's quite pretty,' I'd said. 'Got big eyes, she likes gardening, planting stuff.' I reopened our chat and sent her a picture of the CD.

Me : That's my mum. She's like a singer!
Then I added:
Me : This is an old picture, but she still kind of looks like this.

I examined the features on Suzanna's face. This must have been about fifteen years ago. She was staring up into the light, eyes shining. Inside, there were more pictures of her—laughing under a coconut tree, kicking up a pile of leaves.

It was hard to imagine Suzanna like this. The Suzanna I met seemed to move around in a dream. If she smiled, it was a tight and controlled smile. Everything she did was careful and considered, the same way she wrapped her scarf around her head or fastened a brooch on her blouse. What happened to her?

My phone buzzed with Dessi's SMS.

Dessi : Cool! You look just like her!

Did I? I looked at the CD again. She was definitely darker, and more womanly. I turned back to my phone and forwarded Dessi the video.

Me : This is her song. I can play it!

I was scrolling through my phone, looking for more pictures to send Dessi, when her next message came in.

Dessi : Who's the guy?
Me : Justin. Just some guy I met.

Her reply came in immediately.

Dessi : He's cute.

Chapter 20

Breakthrough

By the time I went back to Suzanna's house, it was almost 1 p.m.

'You're a bit late today,' she commented.

'Yeah, I had some things to do,' I mumbled.

Suzanna didn't mention anything about Pa having been there. I didn't ask.

'Remember the burdock you helped me clean?' she said. 'It's ready!' She drew out a basket and I saw the slices of burdock we had prepared. 'They're all dried up now!' she exclaimed, her eyes shining.

She went to a cupboard and took out a tray of jars. Then she bent down and pulled out some bowls. I watched her arrange everything on the counter. She looked nothing like the woman on the CD cover.

'When did you start wearing a headscarf?' I asked.

Suzanna looked up. 'A few years ago,' she replied.

'Why?'

'I just felt like it,' she shrugged. She placed a few slivers of burdock into a porcelain bowl, added a pinch of this, a dab of that; it was like she was painting.

'Are you some sort of herbalist?' I asked.

'Herbalist,' she repeated. 'I like that word. People just call me *Makcik Su*, the tea maker. If you need something for a headache,

I can help. If you can't sleep, I can make something for that too.'
She smiled. 'There's a herb for everything. Try this.' She placed a
cup of clear green liquid in front of me.

'Mmm,' I said, after taking a sip. 'So what is this good for?'

'It just tastes nice.'

I laughed. 'It does.'

She topped up the teapot with hot water and placed it in the
middle of the table. The steam from it swirled between us like
mist. 'I heard your song,' I announced. 'Ratu.' Suzanna froze, her
elbows perched on the table.

'I didn't know you sang,' I continued. 'You are so good!'

Suzanna still did not respond.

'Can you play something for me?'

She shook her head.

'Why not?'

'I don't do those things anymore.'

'Those things.' Why did she sound so afraid? I remembered
making up different versions of her over the years. From the
jewelled comb in my bedroom, I imagined her as some sort of
queen. From the batik prints in the trunk, I saw that she favoured
deep browns over prissy pinks. I could not picture her as afraid
of anything.

And yet, she now sat glancing at the window as if banshees
were about to fly in. 'Oh, I have the CD,' I said, opening up my
bag. I forgot it was there. I whipped it out and handed it to her.

She looked at it like it was an alien object. Sunshine lit up her
name. There was no mistaking it, despite the brittleness of the
paper or the crack on the cover. A gecko clicked from the ceiling
and Suzanna jumped. She was startled by the smallest thing—
the creak of the fan, the flicker of a curtain. She glanced at the
window again.

I scanned the room and saw an old guitar sitting in the corner.
'Can I use that?' I slipped the guitar out of its case and began

twisting the knobs. The strings vibrated semitone by semitone, until it hit the right key.

'You can play by ear?' Suzanna asked.

I nodded. I plucked out the tune I had learned from Justin. The first verse, the second verse and then the chorus. It'd always been like that with music. It just stuck in my head—sometimes even when I didn't want it to.

I continued playing until I reached the end. When I stopped, Suzanna hadn't moved, she was still holding her cup, but her eyes were brimming with tears. 'I remember it,' I said softly. 'I knew I'd heard it before. Did you write it in Melbourne?'

Suzanna took a deep breath then she let it out slowly.

'That was your song, right?' I asked again.

She sat still for a moment, then she gave the smallest nod—a trigger, a switch—as if she had resolved to do something and that something was to get up and go to the piano. She removed the lace covering, oblivious to the sprinkle of dust that fell to the ground and then she placed her fingers on the keys—tentatively at first, then springing across the board like they had acquired a life of their own. The music surged out and everything stopped to listen—the banana tree, the cat, the sun shining through a cracked window.

After that day, I saw the change. If she was a rock, it would have been some kind of crack in the middle, and the light slipped out like milk. An energy flowed between Suzanna and me, and it carried through to the people in the village. When I came over, the two little girls I had seen on the first day—Mia and Sasha—would wave at me, calling me *Kak Katie* or Big Sister Katie. They handed me flowers and weeds, and I'd make them into daisy chains. Their mothers—who worked at the market—no longer gawked at me. I slipped through the streets like smoke from the satay stalls; like wind through the trees.

Chapter 21

Teacher

Pa was in Ipoh the whole of the week. So I went to Suzanna's house almost every day. She never questioned why I was there or if Pa was okay with it. Perhaps she knew Pa was away and I wondered how often they spoke to each other. In any case, I would just show up at her house, usually at about 11 a.m., and she would be happy to see me.

On Thursday, I didn't go over because I went to Genting Highlands with Roy and Maggie. But on Friday, I turned up again, and she never asked why I hadn't come the day before. She just said, 'Want some chrysanthemum tea?' Then when we finished, she said, 'You're helping today.'

I put down my cup. 'What?'

'Come on,' she said, leading me to a cupboard full of stationery.

Apparently, she tutored some of the village children in English and Malay. At noon, they traipsed in with their pencil cases in hand. It was not like a school. It was more like a random selection of kids aged between four to eight. The girls wore their usual baju kurungs. The boys were in normal shirts, except for one—little Zain, who wore a Superman's cape. Mia and Sasha were there too. They waved at me as they entered.

Suzanna rolled out a mat on the floor and got the children to sit on it. She said something to them in Malay and they giggled. When she pointed at me, they said, '*Selamat Pagi* Puan Suzanna *dan* Cik Katie', meaning 'Good morning, Mrs Suzanna and Miss Katie.' They said it in a sing-song way that made me smile.

I watched Suzanna put up a chart of animal pictures on the whiteboard. She asked the students to write down the names of the animals in Malay. So the children came up one by one to write the words. At the end of it all, everyone read out the words and soon I too knew the Malay words for things like dog, cat, spider and frog.

At break time, Suzanna asked me to help look after Zain while she took the other kids through some grammar. He said something to me in Malay and I smiled, pretending to understand. I tried to think of something to say and the only Malay phrase I could think of was, '*Apa itu?*' which meant 'What is that?' So I pointed to a table and said 'Apa itu?' Zain looked at me with his large shining eyes and said, '*Meja*'.

'Apa itu?' I said, pointing to the door, and he said, '*Pintu*'. We began walking around the house and I learned the words for flower, cup and shoe—and that pencil was still 'pencil' in Malay, or something that sounded like it.

When the group got back together again, Suzanna said, 'Why don't we get Cik Katie to teach us an English song?' Of course, she said this in Malay so I didn't know what the cheer was for. When she repeated it in English, I frowned and cranked my brain. I saw the animal chart on the whiteboard and thought of 'Baa Baa Black Sheep'—but the truth was, I didn't really know all the words to it.

'Errr . . . how about ABBA?' I said, glancing at Suzanna. They had just done an ABBA Throwback at school and I knew the words to that, even some actions. Suzanna pursed her lips, then smiled. 'Yah, why not?'

By the end of the song, the kids gathered around me and yelled, 'ABBA! ABBA! ABBA!' So, I went through the ABBA playlist on my phone and hit play on another song. Their favourite, hands-down, was 'Dancing Queen'. We had two encores that day, with Mia prancing around like a dancing queen herself. After the song ended, Sasha begged, 'One more time? Please?' She was supported by an echo of pleads. I turned to Suzanna but her face was serious. 'No,' she said, clasping her hands together.

'You sure?' I said. 'We still have a few more minutes . . .'

'No,' she said again, her eyes flickering to the window. 'Come on, everyone, get back to the mats. Let's do one more passage from the Quran.'

Suzanna strode to the window and glanced outside. Then she closed one of the shutters and turned back to the room.

* * *

A few days later, we had another 'school' session. Suzanna put up a poster of a rainbow on the board. We were going to do colours that day. I arranged some colouring sheets on the kids' table and took out the colour pencils from the cupboard. I opened up a new pack of Textas (they were called Magic Ink here), thinking Zain might like to use them.

At 9.30 a.m., no one turned up at the door. I looked at my watch. Yes, it was 9.30 a.m. I looked at the clock on the wall and the blacks hands pointed at 9.32 a.m. The mats were laid out. The ceiling fan whirred. At 9.35 a.m., the door still remained shut.

The fan continued to creak above our heads. The curtains fluttered. I picked up the colouring sheets and straightened them out. I went to the craft box and started sorting all the glittery stickers and glue sticks into separate sections. When I finished, I glanced at the clock again. The black hand had moved to 9.45 a.m. and still nobody had showed up.

'What's going on?' I asked.

Suzanna checked her phone, frowning at the screen. Then she turned to me and said they were not coming today.

'All of them?' I said.

'Yes.'

I looked at the mat rolled out on the floor and the sun shining on the activity sheets. 'Why?'

Suzanna glanced at the window and shrugged. 'I'm not sure,' she said. 'Maybe they're sick.'

'I saw the girls this morning, they looked okay.'

Suzanna shrugged. 'It's okay. Let's have some tea then,' she said brightly. She got up and started removing the rainbow poster. I fiddled with the edge of the tablecloth. Suzanna moved around casually—rolling up one mat first, and then another. There was a light smile on her face. I got up and started putting away the colouring sheets.

Chapter 22

Gardening

I was washing the cups when I heard a loud knock on the front door. I heard voices, then footsteps, then Suzanna said, 'Katie, your friend is here.'

What friend? I don't have any friends here. A boy with a mop of curly hair stepped out. 'Hi.' Justin grinned. He looked at Suzanna then back at me, then back at Suzanna as if trying to figure something out.

Suzanna did the same. 'So, you guys know each other from . . .?'

'We play music together,' said Justin glibly.

'Oh, really?' said Suzanna.

'Yes, Katie's really good on the guitar.' He fumbled in his bag and pulled out something. 'My friend is a big fan of yours. Would you please sign this for him?'

Suzanna stared at the CD. It seemed like the sun's rays were slowly eating it up. She let out a weak smile, then she took the pen and signed it. 'Katie was about to help me with some gardening,' she said. 'Do you want to help too?'

'You don't have to!' I gushed at Justin.

'I don't mind, I don't have class until later.'

So Justin put his bag on a chair and followed me outside. I showed him the old vegetable patch we had to clear up.

He surveyed the area with a sweeping glance, the way he did at Pete's Place, as if one look was all it took to absorb every single nuance in the room. 'I'll use this one?' He held up a shovel.

I nodded and watched him step into the garden. 'You came all this way to get her autograph?'

'Nasa's a big fan.' He smiled. I could never tell if he was joking. He twisted his fingers around a vine and yanked it up, the movement echoing how he played the guitar.

'Are you guys playing at the FM18?' I asked, tossing a bunch of weeds away.

Justin froze, holding a vine in mid-air. 'Nope,' he said curtly, before chucking the vine down.

'Why not?'

'Not interested,' he said, wearily.

'Is it because you're with Wira?'

'I told you,' snapped Justin, his face going dark. 'I'm not with Wira!'

'I mean because you live in the village—'

'That doesn't mean I'm with them.' Justin stood up and placed his hands on his hips. 'I don't care what the Wira group do. They can do anything they want and you guys can do anything you want. I'm not involved in any of this.' He scowled. 'Are we doing that patch too?' He yanked up an old onion plant. He did the same with a creeper. After a while, he seemed less agitated. 'Why don't you play?' he asked, his voice now softer.

His face was calmer, the frown had disappeared. 'I can't play in public,' I said. 'Didn't you see me at Pete's Place?'

Justin grinned. 'You were not too bad.'

'I get panic attacks,' I explained. 'I think I've probably failed every single guitar exam I've ever sat for.' I told Justin how I froze up whenever I had to do something in public: like playing at the school concert, or the State Spectacular audition, or even just speaking in front of the class. 'But I'm a bit better now, I've been seeing a psychologist for years.'

'You have a psychologist?'

'Yes, lots of people have them in Melbourne. Don't you?'

'Nope.' Justin stood up to stretch his back. 'I always thought they were for people with . . . well, problems.'

'Not really, anyone can see one. People with stress, anxiety, anger management issues . . .'

'Anger management?' Justin dusted some soil off his gloves. 'Does it work?'

Dessi went to see a psychologist when her parents divorced. She said it was bullshit. 'Sometimes,' I said, tossing a rock away.

The pile between us grew into a small mountain of weeds. 'What's your mum doing with this anyway?' Justin studied the area around us, now clean and clear. 'Is she planting vegetables?'

I told him what Suzanna did with the herbs, how she made special concoctions to heal people. She had lots of different characters coming to the house. People who had sleep problems, someone who wanted to lose weight, someone who wanted more energy. There was a tea for everything.

'Did she cure you as well?' he asked.

'Hm?'

'You don't seem afraid of germs anymore.'

I noticed my hands covered in dirt, my feet half sunken in the soil. Justin was right. I couldn't even remember the last time I had checked my temperature.

'Maybe,' I mused. Since I met Suzanna, I was no longer afraid of dying.

The world just didn't seem so dangerous anymore. The fact that she was alive meant my previous theories about mortality had been wrong. I dusted the dirt off my hands and wiped the sweat off my brow. Crickets chirped in the bushes, a butterfly hovered around a hibiscus. I paused and inhaled the garden air—moist with the scent of warm grass and berries—then I reached out to pull up another bunch of weeds.

When we finished clearing both plots of land, we took the garbage bags to the front of the house. On the way back in, Justin stopped at the verandah. 'What is that?' He pointed to a metal bowl with something mushy and feathery inside, something that looked like a dead bird.

'I don't know,' I said. 'Is it the cat's?'

He took a closer look and his gaze hardened.

'What?' I said.

'Looks like a *jampi*.'

'A what?'

'A spell.'

'For what?'

Justin shrugged. 'Could be anything. You know, like to ward off bad luck or evil spirits . . .'

'You mean there are evil spirits here?' I scanned the trees, suddenly seeing shadows I'd never noticed before.

'No, not in the garden. This one was placed too near the house.'

'What do you mean?'

'I don't know, it's probably nothing.'

'You think Suzanna put it there?'

'No, not her.' said Justin. He spun around and made his way back to the back. Then who? Justin didn't explain any further.

'Do you really believe in this sort of thing?' I asked.

'No, not really.'

Not really. But a tiny bit then? A tiny bit that seemed to show in the stiffness of his shoulders as he walked back to the garden.

* * *

We sat on the terrace, sipping on boxes of sugarcane juice. Me, on a rattan chair. Justin on the other, resting his feet on a stool. I asked him if he was in high school. He said he was in 'college' and was going to university next year. He didn't look quite old enough for university. 'What are you going to study?' I asked.

'Engineering.'

'Do you like engineering?'

'Not really, but my dad thinks I should do it,' Justin muttered under his breath, before looking over to meet my eyes. 'What?'

'You don't really look like an engineer,' I mused.

'What do I look like then?'

'I don't know.' I replied, glancing away, though I thought he looked like an artist or musician. A bee buzzed around and the smell of algae drifted up from the soil we had cleared. My phone beeped, piercing the still, humid air. It was a photo of Dessi in a lacy black dress. Her hair stylishly piled up.

Me	: Are you at the Spring Dance?
Dessi	: Yep. John Ichuda is asking about you.
Me	: Sigh. Wish I was there.
Dessi	: Why haven't you been replying to his messages?
Me	: I have. I've just been a bit busy with Suzanna and all.

The days had gone by so quickly. It seemed like there was not enough time to see her. And I always had to do it between going out with Tua Ee and Roy and Pa, or telling them I was off to study. It was exhausting running around like this.

| Dessi | : Are you sure you still like him? ☺ |

A fly landed on my knee and flew off. I thought of the day John Ichuda and I had walked back from the library together. It had started raining and we had stopped under a blue gum tree. That was the moment when a small seed of hope began to bloom, with him towering next to me as waited for the rain to stop.

When I didn't reply, Dessi's message came in again.

Dessi   : Do you??

It was hard to tell what her expression was. Was she seriously curious or was she kidding?

'Is it that guy friend who's just a friend?' said Justin.

'What?'

Justin smiled and gestured at my phone.

'No, that was Dessi,' I replied. I cleared my throat and watched the bamboo chimes dancing above my head. I told him about John Ichuda. We'd met at the scholarship class. He played the saxophone. He also played tennis for school. He wanted to work for the Boston Consulting Group and did volunteer work with homeless kids on the side.

'Is there anything this guy doesn't do?'

I laughed. 'Not really.'

'I like how you call him "John Ichuda",' said Justin. 'Like he can't just be "John".'

'That's true.' I laughed.

There was a light pattering sound on the roof. 'Looks like rain,' commented Justin. 'We still have a bit more to go, don't we?'

I scanned the curtain of drizzle. 'Maybe it's just a passing shower.'

'Passing shower?' Justin said, quizzically. He stared at me for a moment and said, 'Yeah, probably just a passing shower. We should just wait it out.'

I grabbed my tote back from the table and whipped out a book. I opened it out to the marked page. 'What are you reading?' Justin asked, chuckling. 'Is that a science textbook?'

'Yeah.' I held it up so he could see 'Year 11 Biology' on the cover.

'Is it good?'

'Yeah,' I nodded, trying to interpret his expression. 'I always have a book with me. I hate being idle.'

'Idle . . .' He smiled again.

'What?' I felt like I was missing a joke.

Justin took a deep breath and beamed at the sky. 'It's good to be idle sometimes,' he said, stretching out his arms. He squinted into the distance and said, 'Can you see that?'

'What?'

'The trees.' He pointed at some fir trees beyond the fence.

'They're moving,' I said.

'Yes, but look at the light around it.'

I noticed then the pale pink glow emanating from its branches. 'What is that?' I asked.

Justin shrugged. 'It happens in the evening sometimes, when the air is very humid.'

I watched the rain continue to beat down on the plants and the way some leaves caught hold of the water. Each pore sparkled with a water droplet, making the whole tree shimmer like silver.

Justin leaned towards me, close enough for me to smell a soap-like scent from his shirt.

'What are you doing?' I said.

'You have glitter all over your skin.'

'Oh, it must have been from the craft box earlier,' I mumbled, wiping my wrist.

'You have a star.' Justin said. He reached out to peel the sticker off my blouse.

'Oh, so that's where it went,' I said, my cheeks flushing. 'You can have it.' He peered at the sticker on my finger—a piece of foam sprinkled with silver dust—and chucked it into his bag. We spent the rest of the hour talking about everything and nothing in particular. From time to time, I checked my phone but there were no more messages from Dessi and I could only imagine the fun she was having there.

* * *

After Justin left, Suzanna and I sat at the dining table sorting out some herbs. The evening had cooled and the shadows made long sleepy stretches on the concrete.

'So, this Justin guy seems nice.' Suzanna snipped off a piece of coriander.

'Yes, he's quite friendly.'

'Does he like you?'

'No.' I laughed. I told her he was probably going out with this girl called Tina, who was gorgeous.

'Really?'

'Yeah, why?'

Suzanna shrugged. 'How about you? Do you like anyone?'

'No,' I replied. 'Well, there is this guy . . .' I told her about John Ichuda and our potential relationship.

'I think you just know when you meet your soulmate,' Suzanna said.

Soulmate. Wow, I'm not sure I'd thought of John Ichuda in that way. Handsome? Yes. Lying down against his broad, muscular shoulders? Mm-hm.

'You believe in soulmates?' I asked.

'Of course.' Suzanna said this with the certainty of someone who had sought these answers before. 'Although,' she added. 'I think you have different soulmates at different points in your life.'

The wind creaked through the cracks in the house. The lace curtains fluttered. Is that what happened with her and Pa? Was Pa just a phase in her life? I scanned the room and noted the two brown mugs drying on a rack. A leather spectacle case on the bookshelf. 'How come you are so close to Tun Said?'

Suzanna explained they were friends from childhood. He went to the UK for university and when he came back, they continued to stay in touch.

'Did you guys ever go out?' I asked.

'No, we are just friends.'

Was that hesitation in her voice? We continued speaking like this in the silence of the afternoon, my mother and I—about the future and the past, about the people we were before. Of course, it didn't make up for all those times I'd walked home alone, or stood alone at a birthday party or stared at my bedroom ceiling wondering about the missing gap in my life. But this—this sitting here in the middle of an old wooden house as the fan creaked over our heads—was more than I'd ever imagined. The shadows stretched along the concrete, the smell of coriander swirled around us, and I knew I never wanted to lose her again.

Chapter 23

Missing

The next time I stepped into Kampung Damai, there was a flurry of activity. A Wira soldier raced up to a wall and tore a poster off. A young girl scurried across the street without stopping to pick up the ball she dropped. 'What's going on?' I questioned a man rushing by. He wore a white skull cap and was clutching a shopping bag. 'Haven't you heard?' he said. 'They're doing a raid.'

'What raid?' I asked, but the man had disappeared. A loud screeching sound pierced the air, winding up to a crescendo. From the horizon, I saw about fifty motorbikes appear. They tore down the streets like locusts, weaving in and out of the lanes. In the distance, a lorry creaked, a lumbering giant pulling its weight up the road.

Two men parked their motorbikes in front of a house. They took off their helmets and scrutinized the area. Mak Minah from the convenience store crept up beside me. I shifted my foot, careful not to step on the hem of her sarong. 'What are they doing?' I whispered.

She put a finger to her lips and we both peered through the bamboo leaves. A man strutted down the driveway and rapped on the door. When it opened, he went inside. A few minutes later, he came out carrying a large cardboard box. A woman clung to his elbow, pleading him to stop but he kept walking down the driveway.

'What are they doing?' I asked Mak Minah again.

'They are taking . . .' she paused, as if searching for the word, 'the forbidden things.'

The guy with the box ran up to the lorry and emptied it into the back. The items fell into the carriage with a crash. I heard the bang of metal on metal and the tinkle of something porcelain breaking. The second guy came out from another house and dumped some items into a roadside bin. A pile of magazines fell out. I saw the titles: *Marie Claire, Her World, Glamour.* A feeling of unease came over me as I thought of Suzanna and her encyclopaedia collection. As soon as the truck left, I hurried over to her house.

When I reached the front gate, I noticed how quiet the whole place was. The curtains that were usually fluttering were still, the window shutters were closed. Even the banana tree stood unmoving, as if it was pretending to be dead to the world. I ran up the porch and knocked on the candy pink door. Nothing, no footsteps or cooking sounds. No scent of anything. Just a smear of rust around the latch. I walked back down and saw the cat slinking behind a bush. A row of giant yams stirred in the wind, one leaf nudging the next and then that leaf nudging the next one. Behind the last plant, I saw a girl huddled in white.

'Mia,' I said, 'What are you doing?'

Her eyes grew wide. She tried to hide the CD in her hand but I had already seen it. It was Suzanna's name peeping out from underneath her fingers.

'Where did you get that?' I demanded.

She glanced at Sasha standing beside her.

'Did Puan Suzanna give it to you?' I asked, gentler this time.

Mia clutched the CD more tightly.

'It's okay,' I assured her. 'I'm not angry. I'm just looking for her.'

Mia glanced at Sasha again. Then she pointed to a large bin by the gate. It was so full, the lid looked like a beret perched on top of a mountain of things: CDs, books, an old cassette player with a radio antenna sticking out. I asked Mia if she had seen Suzanna. She shook her head vigorously, clamming her mouth shut till it formed a tight line.

'Do you know where Puan Suzanna is?' I asked Sasha. She looked at Mia, Mia looked at me, then she said, 'She went into the Wira car.'

'Where did they take her?'

Mia glanced at Sasha again, then turned back to me. Her words came out as a whisper. '*Sungai Besi*,' she replied.

'What?' I said. 'What is that?'

Mia and Sasha had already started running off, two white figures disappearing behind the fence. 'Wait,' I called out. 'Wait, what did you say?'

I ran to the gate and someone grabbed my elbow. 'Get down,' he whispered. I found myself face to face with Justin, his breath warm against my cheek. He pointed towards the road and I saw the lorry rolling towards us, accompanied by a flock of motorcycles on either side.

Chapter 24

Nasa's House

After all the Wira soldiers had left, I got into Justin's car and he started driving to Nasa's house. 'So you know this place?' Sue-ngai . . . Sue-ngai . . .'

'Sungai Besi,' he said. 'It's a rehabilitation centre.'

'Rehabilitation from what?'

Justin kept his eyes on the wheel. 'Riana will tell you,' he replied. Riana was Nasa's sister and had been there before. That's all Justin revealed. Suzanna's CD was still in my hand. I slipped it into my bag and clutched the strap tightly.

'I'm not sure why they would take her, though,' said Justin.

'Is it because they found her CDs?'

'Other people had banned stuff too. They just take the stuff.' Justin frowned at the road. 'Maybe it's something else.'

'What do you mean?'

Justin shrugged. 'Could it be the songs? I heard you've been teaching kids some songs that might be . . . inappropriate.'

'Inappropriate? It's ABBA! Is that inappropriate?'

Justin's face remained grim. 'To some people, it may be. Any English music is considered evil.'

'What? Even nursery rhymes?'

'Maybe. These are not your usual bunch of people. If you're teaching their kids anything 'Western', you might be seen as a 'bad influence'. People here like to keep their kids away from anything foreign—movies, books, chewing gum; they may even think you are a threat.'

'Me? Why?'

I looked down at myself. I'd made an effort to be appropriately covered, these days. I wore a white, long-sleeved linen shirt and a long beige skirt. 'Is it my clothes?'

Justin cleared his throat. 'No. It's just that you don't look exactly local.' It hit me then. The jampi on the deck. The warning to stay away. Was it for me? Was I the 'evil spirit'? It occurred to me then that Suzanna was likely in trouble because of me. Harbouring a threat . . . an evil influence. The seatbelt across my chest felt tight. 'How much longer till we get there?' I asked.

'Maybe half an hour.'

* * *

Justin turned into a housing estate that seemed very new. The words next to the guardhouse said *'Medan Serai'*—gold letters on black marble. Some of the houses were still under construction and trucks rolled up and down the streets. We drove past a roundabout with a giant hibiscus sculpture, a row of 'logs' made of cement. There were a lot of these fake 'natural' things around and I wondered why they couldn't just use real logs.

We stopped at house number twenty-seven. Justin didn't ring the bell. He pushed the side gate open and strolled right onto the porch. He knocked on the door and it opened, revealing a girl in a peach headscarf. 'Hi Riana,' Justin said, his voice, warm and friendly.

Riana stayed silent. She opened the door wider and let us in.

'Where's Nasa?' Justin scanned the room. 'He's supposed to meet us here.'

Riana did not reply. She simply drifted to a window where a thick book lay open on the table. When the sunlight fell on her face, I realized who she was. She wasn't wearing a grey robe like on the day of the beating but she had the same pale face. Devoid of any jewellery—not an earring or a bracelet in sight—there was a certain pureness about the way she titled her head or gazed out the window. I couldn't help staring at the back of her blouse. Were there scars? Was she hurt? She shifted her ankles and her long skirt skimmed the floor.

Nasa appeared with a big smile on his face. 'Sorry,' he said. 'Was in the shower.' He glanced at Riana and told us, 'She's in one of her moods again.' He went over to her. 'Hey,' he called. 'Can we ask you something about Sungai Besi?'

Riana's head remained bent over the book.

'My friend Katie needs to go there.' He pointed at me. Riana paused, her finger stopping in the middle of a line then just as I thought she was going to say something, she continued reading again.

Nasa came back to us in the living room and shrugged. 'What's she reading?' I asked.

'The Quran. It's like the Bible.'

'Does she do that a lot?'

'She's been like this since . . .' his words trailed off. 'Yes, she does,' he finished.

Nasa pried open a tin of biscuits and offered it to us. 'Are you sure your mum is in Sungai Besi?' he said.

'Yes, why?'

'I spoke to a friend and they said no one went to Sungai Besi.'

'I'm pretty sure she went there.' I recalled Mia's earnest expression and the way she had whispered the words.

'Most people go to *Gombak*,' explained Nasa. 'Only the more serious cases are handled at Sungai Besi.'

'What do you mean more serious? What happens there?'

Nasa scratched the side of his eyebrow. 'It's a rehabilitation centre,' he said. 'You go there to get better . . .'

'To get better from what?'

Nasa gave Riana another glance. 'She went there after getting caught for doing something. She . . .' Nasa struggled to finish.

'I saw her,' I said. 'I saw her get beaten.'

'Yes.' Nasa's eyes hardened. 'She went there after that. She was there for two weeks. And then she came back . . . like this.'

'What did they do to her there?'

Nasa turned to Justin. 'Why can't you get her in?'

'You know I hate going there,' replied Justin. 'What did you do when Riana was there? Could you visit her?'

'Nope.' Nasa shook his head. 'No visits. Even my mum couldn't go see her. It's kind of like a "retreat". They took her handphone and said she couldn't call or speak to anyone.'

'That's crazy, it sounds like a jail,' I said.

'A little bit.'

'How is that legal? Couldn't you call the police?'

'They operate like the police,' said Nasa.

'The law in the village is a little bit different,' explained Justin. 'They follow their own interpretations of the Shariah law.'

'What did they do to her in there?' I asked.

Nasa pinched his lip. 'To be honest, I don't really know. Riana doesn't like talking about it and we don't ask. She came back very quiet, a bit dazed. She didn't want to go out with her usual friends anymore.'

I needed to get Suzanna out of there. She shouldn't be there. 'Can you take me there?' I asked Justin.

'No,' he replied. 'What are you going to do? Just march up and say she shouldn't be there?'

'Yes, something like that. I think she's there because of me—'

'Katie,' said Justin. 'I told you, things work differently here. Once she's in there, you can't get her out—not formally, at least.'

'What do you mean?'

'I need to talk to Nasa about something. Why don't you grab some water from the kitchen?'

* * *

I needed to get Suzanna out. It was my fault. The CDs, the music, the piano—that was all me. I was the one who had got her into trouble. I found the water next to the fridge as Nasa had explained and poured myself a glass. Just as I put the kettle down, Riana walked in. She leaned against the counter and tilted her head.

'Have we met before?' She narrowed her eyes at me. I thought of the crowd that day and the man swinging up his cane. I cleared my throat. 'I may have seen you at Kampung Damai the other day . . . erm, at the Wira building.'

'You were there, were you?' Riana picked up the kettle and poured out a shaky stream of water. Her baju kurung had a strange whispery quality that made her seem like a light silvery being. 'Why did they do that to you?' I asked softly.

Riana had the most beautiful skin, so smooth and flawless that anything she did seemed to wrinkle her complexion in some way. I watched her bring the glass away from her mouth and wipe away a tiny drop of water.

'I was seeing someone I was not allowed to,' she said softly.

'A guy?'

She nodded.

'What was wrong with him?'

'Nothing. It's just that we were not married,' she replied as if that explained everything.

I sipped the water in my glass. It had a slight metallic taste to it. Would they do that to Suzanna because of Pa? Because he was not Muslim?

'Why do you want to go there?' Riana said suddenly.

'My mother is there.'

Riana lowered her eyes. She had thick, beautiful lashes, like one of those dolls that closed their eyes when you laid them down. 'I need to get her out,' I continued.

'She will come out eventually.'

My mind began to fill with all kinds of images. I imagined a prison, a jail, solitary confinement like in a war movie. Or was it like a mental institution where they tied you to your bed?

'What did they do to you there?' I asked.

'They didn't do anything. You eat, you sleep, you think about life.' There was a pause. A drop of water clung to the rim of the tap before it splashed into the sink. 'They help you find your way,' she said. 'For those who are lost, they will be found. Allah leads you to the path of righteousness.' Riana's voice had taken on a strange dream-like quality. 'It will be fine,' she said. 'He will lead us all to the path that is set out for us.' She gave me a blank smile and nodded politely. It was as if she had turned into someone else.

* * *

When I got back to the living room, Justin and Nasa were still hunched over the sofa. 'I think I can get us in through the kitchen,' Justin said. 'I know some people there.'

'But the women's area is on the other side,' mused Nasa. 'You have to go through the main section to get there.'

'How about the back route near the offices?'

'That could work, then you bring her back through the kitchen?'

Justin nodded. 'But how do I get to the office area without being seen?'

A bulldozer droned in the distance. I had nothing to say as I had no idea what the place looked like. Maybe it had high walls and electric fences, guards patrolling all over the place. Justin and Nasa continued to talk. The lady on the TV raved about a laundry detergent that could remove mud stains. Then out of nowhere, above the hum of it all, Riana said, 'You can go through the courtyard. They leave the garden doors unlocked.'

Chapter 25

Rescue Mission

Justin and I drove on Highway 61 towards Sungai Besi. The Rainforest unfurled before us on either side. Blankets of it; an impenetrable Jurassic forest, millions of years old. This was a real jungle, not bush or scrub like the Dandenongs. The forest here was so thick, you could only imagine the creatures within—tigers, monkeys, snakes the size of crocodiles.

Melbourne seemed a million miles away. There were so many things here I didn't understand. The events of the past few days rolled by like scenes outside my window. While KL City seemed like a metropolis light years ahead, some parts of it felt stuck in time.

'Why did they do that to Riana?' I said. 'You know . . . the beating . . .'

'It's Shariah law, according to them,' Justin said with a shrug.

'What did she do that was so wrong?'

'They were holding hands.'

'You mean you're not allowed to hold hands?'

'Not in the village.'

'But it's okay elsewhere?'

Justin smiled. 'As long as you don't get caught.' He curved the car around a bend and I wondered if he had ever held hands with a girl. Of course he had. I watched the way his curls fell over his jaw, that dimple on his cheek.

We drove through a tunnel and came out the other side. The scenery began to change. A banana plantation, a paddy field, a broken bus-stop sign. 'Let's get a drink,' Justin said.

'What? Where?'

There was nothing around us except for grassy fields. A truck roared beside us, carrying about a hundred chicken coops in the back. As it pulled ahead, Justin gestured towards a small wooden shelter on the right.

'Is that a shop?' I squinted at the structure far away.

'Yeah, it looks good.'

I was not sure how he could tell. The stall looked like a hut in the middle of nowhere, a blue tarpaulin covering one side. We parked on gravel, got out and started making our way across a field. I followed Justin's footsteps but when I got to a muddy section, I stopped. 'Cross over there.' He pointed at a log.

'Here.' His hand lay outstretched and waiting.

Could he feel the sweat of my palm? I could picture every curve and line on his. I'd never really held a boy's hand before, except for those few minutes with Ryan White—and that was more like gripping the elbow of his suit as we kissed. I felt my cheeks grow hot. I concentrated on navigating the dents on the log, looking out for slippery mossy bits. When I reached the other side, I jumped off and quickly let go.

The stall was literally a shelter held up by poles. It reminded me of that time I went camping with Dessi and her mother's friend—the way the poles would wobble in the wind and hot air would squeeze between the flaps. It wasn't unpleasant. In fact, it was kind of refreshing living amidst nature, knowing that the sea was just on the other side.

The stall gave off a similar vibe. It made me feel like I was in the last restaurant in the universe. An Indian man stood behind a stove, tossing a ball of dough onto a hot plate. He flipped it out like playdough, so swiftly and quickly, it looked like magic. He did this a few times, prompting me to catch the hidden card, the secret move but it happened so fast, and soon the dough became light and fluffy, sizzling on the pan.

'Let's sit there.' Justin gestured to one of the plastic tables. He grabbed a stool and I saw a tattoo above his elbow. What was it—a flower, a fish? He didn't seem like the kind of person to have a tattoo. I couldn't imagine him with any earrings or piercings, he didn't even wear a watch; it was as if his cotton T-shirt and pants were all he needed in the world.

'Do you want teh tarik?' he said.

'Is that tea?'

'Mm-hm.'

'Okay,' I said and he went over to order. The Indian man poured out the tea from one billy can into another. He stretched out the liquid so far apart, it looked like a long piece of brown silk. Justin stood in front of him, waiting. His T-shirt was slate, his hair was black. He had a beautifully ominous quality about him that made me want to keep staring. I could see why girls liked him.

I thought of the way he held my hand earlier and wondered if he was like that with everyone. Something vibrated on the table and I saw his phone flashing with the name Tina Rahman. The phone buzzed again—but this time only once—leaving some words on the front: 'I miss you', it said. No, it said '1 missed call'.

Justin appeared beside me holding a plastic bag filled with murky brown liquid.

'Is that the tea?' I said.

'Yes.'

'It's in a bag,' I said, eyeing the item suspiciously.

'Yes.'

Justin gave me a funny half-smile. I took the bag from him, holding it like it was a stray kitten or a fish that might bite. I put my finger through the bright pink string and adjusted the straw. 'Have you had curry puffs before?' Justin motioned to the plate between us.

'Of course,' I said as if I ate curry puffs every day. Truth was, I'd only had them once when Diana had bought a frozen pack from Woolies. I picked up the little half-moon pastry and bit into it. A fire filled my mouth. These were not like the Woolies ones at all. 'You okay?' said Justin, smiling.

'Yeah.' I blinked back some tears and took a sip of iced tea. 'It's good.'

It really was. Spicy, yes, and burned my tongue, but every time I took a sip of tea, it all became superbly delicious—a strange blend of pain and sweetness. I took another bite, and another, and soon, I was licking the last piece off my fingers when my phone went 'Ding'. A message from Diana; Diana sitting in her office in Prahran, where there were no rainforests or roadside shacks or people drinking tea out of bags.

Diana   : Have you seen your dad? He hasn't been returning my messages.

I thought of Pa and Suzanna in the house that day. Diana sitting, waiting, immaculate in a creamy silk blouse, while Pa waltzed around the city with Suzanna, chatting and laughing—or dishing out embraces 'What's wrong?' said Justin.

'Nothing.' I studied the container of cutlery in front of me. One fork was slightly bent.

Diana   : Is everything okay?
Me   : Yeah, it's fine.

The moment I pressed Send, I felt the guilt sting my finger.

'Are you sure you're okay?' said Justin.

'Yeah, why?'

'You just sighed.'

'I did?' I pressed the straw between my fingers. 'It's just relationships . . . they're complicated.'

'John Ichuda?'

'No, that was Diana.' I absently stirred the ice in my bag. Justin did not question me further. He just patiently sipped on his drink. 'Did you ever realize that your parents don't really have the answers to things?' I said. 'That they are probably just as clueless as us?'

'I'm not clueless,' Justin smiled.

'Okay. What I meant was when we were young, we thought they knew everything, but the truth is there really is no right or wrong.'

'Ah, so you've only realized this now? It's called the Theory of Maturity.'

'Is there really such a thing?' I made a mental note to look it up.

'No, I just made that up.' Justin grinned and took a big sip from his bag.

* * *

A deep sound rumbled from far away. There was a denseness in the air, almost sweet, like fairy floss. 'It's going to rain at four,' said Justin, looking at his watch.

'How do you know?' I asked.

'It rains at four every day. It's monsoon season, haven't you noticed?'

I tilted my head. 'Not really.'

'It usually lasts for a few hours. It's always like this during this time of the year.'

I thought about the day Justin had helped me in Suzanna's garden. Had he known then it wasn't going to be a passing shower? 'What are you thinking about?' he asked.

I looked at him, a shine in my eyes. 'So, you don't think this will be a passing shower?'

Justin hesitated for a second and replied, 'No'.

The rain started to fall like stones, drumming on the zinc roof. Justin stood up and adjusted the flap of the tarpaulin. At first, I saw a tight, lean abdomen, then I noticed the mark above his elbow. It was neither a flower of a fish. 'What's that?' I said.

'Nothing.' He sat back down.

'Are you hurt?'

'No,' he replied tersely, folding his arms.

'What happened?'

'My dad just does stuff sometimes.'

'What do you mean? Does he hit you?'

Justin shrugged and replied in a clipped voice, 'Sometimes'.

I frowned. How could he be so calm? Was this another cultural thing I didn't understand? What had his father used to cause a scar like that? A cane, a cigarette, his bare hands? The image of his scar remained in my head. I wondered what other scars he had.

A buzz pierced the air. I knew that sound. We both looked at Justin's phone on the table. 'Is that Tina?' I said as he scanned the text.

'Yeah. How did you know?'

'I think she messaged earlier.'

'Oh.' He slipped the phone back into his bag.

'You guys going out?'

'No.'

'Why not? I think you guys would make a really good couple.'

Justin took a sip of tea and peered into the distance.

'She's really pretty,' I said.

'Yes, she is.'

Sunlight shone through the tarpaulin sheet and cast us in a strange blue glow. It felt like we were underwater. Light shadowy specks danced on Justin's face and for a moment, I felt like it was just him and me in some aquarium. When his gaze flicked towards me, I quickly looked away. I could sense he was studying the skyline too.

'A storm is coming,' he said. He was right, the sky had turned quite dark. There was a large cloud shaped like a dragon hanging over the hills. As I sipped the last of my tea, the sky cracked open and an avalanche of water poured out. It shot down everything in its path—the pebbles, the concrete, the shiny rocks on the ground—and ricocheted towards us.

Justin moved his chair closer to mine and tucked his shoes in—these black-and-white checked slip-ons, which looked simply ridiculous, like a cartoon, especially with that picture of a skull on the front and yet, they were kind of cute as well. I could see his lips, soft and red; the curve of his jaw. I thought of him shovelling in the garden, driving beside me in the car—was he like this with everyone?

Could he possibly . . . like me? No, he had Tina. But still. The back of his hand hovered inches away from mine. Was I the only one that felt this current between us? A whiff of cigarette smoke, the smell of wet grass. Did he feel it too? If he took my hand, it would be a sign that he did. The rain roared like a crowd watching. I moved my little finger an inch closer. There was nothing stopping him now, all he needed to do was breathe in my direction. His hand lingered for two seconds—I felt the sizzle of its closeness—then he swiftly moved it away.

Chapter 26

Sungai Besi

The Sungai Besi Rehabilitation Centre hardly looked like the fortress I had imagined it to be. Magenta-coloured bougainvillaea cascaded over the front wall like the lobby of a resort in St Moritz. There were flagpoles upfront, waving three different flags: the Malaysian flag, the state flag and the green Wira flag. Justin slid his Honda Civic into a parking spot. We stepped out and went straight to the boot. Justin took out two boxes with the words 'Amart' printed boldly on each side. He gave one box to me and grabbed another for himself. When he handed me mine, our knuckles grazed and I could still feel the touch of it even after.

We'd picked up the groceries from a supermarket in Kampung Damai. Apparently, they were the centre's monthly order. We stood there with our boxes in front of the gleaming white building. Everything was white—the walls, the window sills, the textured balustrades—making the cascade of magenta flowers pop out even more. Justin scanned the building as if he were tracing an outline of it in his head then he took a deep breath and stepped forward.

I followed him up a path towards the main entrance and when we reached the foyer, a Wira guard stopped us, tall and glassy, like a gate himself. 'Assalamulaikum,' Justin greeted him, and the man seemed to soften a little. Justin continued in Malay and the man surveyed the boxes—the tins of sardines and coconut jam, condensed milk and Gardenia bread—then he narrowed his eyes at me. I swallowed a ball of saliva and returned his gaze with a smile I hoped was neutral and innocent. Was he wondering why the delivery person this month looked different? Could he see I wasn't even Malaysian? I could feel my palms sweating, my heart pounding out of my chest. I smiled again and Justin said something to the guy that made him chuckle. 'Ho, ho, ho,' the guy said like Santa Claus.

If Justin had a superpower, I think it would be the ability to disarm someone. Disarm—even the word sounded magical—the ability to make someone put their arms away, let their guard down. That is exactly what he seemed to have done to the Wira personnel right now. It didn't matter if the other person was a monster, a tiger, or an enemy in camouflage—like the Wira soldier in front of us—Justin could defuse any situation with laughter.

The guy let us through and we continued on our way around the side of the building. Justin strode down a corridor and went up a garden path. 'You seem to know your way around,' I commented. Justin didn't reply. He pushed away a fern leaf and continued walking. I saw a Wira soldier near a pavilion, peering at us. I gripped my box tightly and kept my head down. If Justin saw him, he gave no indication, he just strode on ahead as if he owned the place.

When we stepped into a courtyard, Justin stopped, examining the tree in the corner. There were about half a dozen lemons on it, ripe and chilling under the overcast sky. 'What is it?' I asked.

'Nothing.' He continued towards a side door and knocked. A lady in a black hijab answered. She barely looked at him—she saw the boxes and reached out for them. 'Selamat pagi, makcik!' Justin greeted her. At the sound of his voice, she looked up.

When she registered his presence, her whole face lit up. She squeezed his hands and ushered him inside, drawing him in like he was a little kid and not a boy who was a foot taller than her. He told me the lady's name was Puan Zainab. She smiled at me kindly and beckoned me inside as well. Two other ladies bustled over and took our boxes away. They wore pastel-coloured headscarves that matched their pastel-coloured baju kurungs. The lady in mauve began to unpack the boxes. The lady in mint went to a counter and resumed slicing some cucumber.

Puan Zainab came over and offered me a cookie from a jar. She didn't say anything, just nudged the jar towards me with a chuckle. '*Terima kasih*,' I said carefully. She chuckled again and I wondered if I had pronounced it wrongly. The lady in mauve slid beside me. 'You speak Malay?'

I shook my head.

'He's grown so much,' she said in English. 'How did you get him to come?'

'When did you last see him?'

'Maybe five years ago. He used to come here when he was young,' she said. 'His mother would drop him off before going to the main office to work. He used to play outside over there.' She gestured towards the lemon tree outside. The sun had broken out and created a slice of sunshine under the tree where I imagined a bundle of toy cars and trucks. The lady continued to look fondly at Justin.

'Why did he stop coming?' I asked.

'Well, when his mother stopped working here, he stopped too. We told his father he would always be welcome here and asked him to bring him along anytime. But I heard he didn't want to come back here anymore.' The lady studied my face. 'Are you his girlfriend?'

'Oh no,' I said, feeling my neck grow hot. 'We are just friends.'

She tilted her head, as if she was going to say something else but in the end, she picked up a plate to dry. Justin and Puan Zainab continued to speak to each other like a reunited aunt and nephew. She pulled him to the stove and asked him to fix something in the cooker hood, a light perhaps. He bent down to peer into it, his T-shirt accentuating the curves of his lean and taut body.

I scanned the kitchen, which was a hum of activity. Everywhere I looked, something seemed to be bubbling or steaming or chopping. The smell of coconut rice filled the air. I suspected it came from the rice cooker in the corner—which, for the record, was the most enormous rice cooker I'd ever seen in my life, the size of a laundry tub.

Soon, Justin said goodbye and we went out through another door. The hallway was dimly lit and I watched Justin studying the corridor. 'So how do you know them?' I asked.

'Just some family friends,' he said, looking left and right.

'One of the ladies told me your mum used to work here. Where is she now?'

'She left.'

Yes, obviously. Before I could ask anything else, Justin said, 'Let's go this way.' He pointed to a corridor on the right. He walked slowly now as if listening or looking for something. Near the end of the corridor, we heard footsteps and pressed ourselves up against a wall. A group of women walked past, singing some Islamic song that echoed through the walls. We passed door-after-door until we reached a corridor that split into two.

'Hm,' said Justin. 'I thought it would be here.' Riana had told us to look for a frosted glass door. But I had seen nothing like that. Justin said he would check out the left corridor. 'Wait here,' he said. 'I'll be back in five minutes.'

Water gurgled from the pipes inside the wall. It was like another world lay within it. It reminded me of a kids' programme I used to watch, *Fraggle Rock*, where a whole city of creatures lived underneath a house without the owners knowing. Five minutes went by and Justin hadn't returned. I took a few steps down the other corridor and heard a sound, a kind of hiccup or a sneeze. Was that Suzanna?

I followed the curve of the corridor and the sound grew louder. Laughing? No, it was crying. In the semi-darkness, I heard long, sobbing sounds coming from a faded door ahead. The lady wailed gently, a wail that was then followed by a long intake of breath. This happened a few times. I imagined Suzanna crumpled on the floor in that room. What had they done to her? Had she suffered a beating? Was she hurt?

I was about to push the door open when I heard scuffling sounds. Footsteps. I quickly ducked into the nearest corridor I could find. It led to another, and then another, and soon I was lost, no longer sure where I was. All the rooms looked the same to me. Fluorescent lights hummed on the ceilings. The walls groaned with squeaks and thuds.

Then at the end of a corridor, I saw a frosted glass door.

The sun shone through it like a rectangle of light; an entrance to salvation. I whipped out my phone and messaged Justin. 'Sending failed,' the screen said. The reception bar was at zero. Voices drifted in from a nearby room. The sound of chairs being folded up. I scanned the corridor. In each direction there seemed to be a brightly lit walkway with nowhere to hide. There was only one way to go. I ran towards the frosted door and slipped outside.

It was just like Riana had described. A shady courtyard with a small fountain in the middle. All around me, plants curled and leaned and stretched upwards. A particularly lush bamboo plant posed at the end of the courtyard with white-speckled leaves. And in-between those leaves, I spotted the other glass door.

I slowly snuck through the trees until I reached the door. I pressed down on the handle but it wouldn't budge. I pushed harder. Maybe it was some kind of fire exit. I gave the door another shove with my shoulder and something snapped at the bottom.

I stood in a hallway, facing a wall, and in a room on my right, I found myself face-to-face with Tun Said. He sat at a desk, looking up at me, his pen poised in mid-air.

Chapter 27

Found

'I thought it was you.' He motioned to the window and I saw it opened straight out into the garden. I could see the fountain and the white-speckled tree. He must have seen everything. 'It's Katie, right?' he said, clicking his pen shut.

I nodded, a lump forming in my throat.

'What are you doing here?' he asked. His Malay shirt was carefully ironed, not a crease in sight. 'I'm looking for Suzanna,' I said, trying not to let my voice shake. I had a flashback of the guy hitting Riana and I could feel the sting on my back. I blinked back my fear and kept my gaze on him.

'She's not here—'

'I know she is,' I said, my voice cracking. 'Where is she? If you don't—'

'She's not on this side, she's in Block B.'

'Oh,' I said.

'It's not far, I can take you.'

I frowned at the affability of his words.

'Let me just finish something first.' He scribbled in a notebook; I could hear the sound of pen scratching on paper. His words rang in my ears. 'It's not far, I can take you.' He had a hint of a British accent. It was hard to imagine that this was the guy speaking to the crowds in Malay the other day.

His moustache, peppered with grey and white, was perfectly trimmed. The cuffs of his sleeves fell perfectly over each of his wrists. Everything about him seemed so exact and precise, it scared me. When we met the other day, we had barely spoken, simply nodding to each other before Suzanna sent me on my way. Now he was looking up at me with beady eyes that seemed to pierce through my brain. 'You are from Melbourne, right?'

'Yes,' I said softly. The lump had disappeared from my throat and my heart was no longer pounding.

'How are things there?' he said with a slight smile and my pulse slowed down some more.

'You've been there?' I asked.

'Yes, I did a postgraduate course at Melbourne Uni.'

'I see.'

I studied the room filled with intellectual-sounding books such as *The Economics of the Human Race*, *The Rise and Fall of Ancient Civilizations*—everything perfectly arranged. Even his pen holder seemed perfect with three blue pens in it, lying evenly apart.

'Are you enjoying your stay here?' Tun Said asked.

'It's . . . different.'

'Yes, life is very different here, isn't it?' Tun Said smiled, his moustache moving up with his mouth. 'I would say it's more civilized. Here, we are very clear on what happens if you disobey God's will. Everyone knows the consequences when you do things that are prohibited. It's very simple, really. You break the rules, you get punished.'

'What about free speech and human rights?'

'What about it?' Tun Said burst into laughter. 'You are definitely from Australia. I know in Melbourne, you are very free. But what I found was . . . freedom breeds chaos. Over here, you don't have many drunk people on the street or people taking drugs. You know why? We simply don't allow it. They know it's evil.'

I thought of the raid; the truck full of stuff. 'So things like magazines and books. Are those things evil too?'

'You have to draw the line somewhere. You have to start with the very root of evil. If you push back, other people will push more and soon, things will get out of control. This is our way,' said Tun Said, bringing his hand to his chest, almost apologetically.

This guy was crazy. There must have been a misunderstanding. 'Why did you take Suzanna?' I said. 'She didn't do anything. Was it the music and the CDs? Those were my things. Please let her go, she didn't do anything.'

Tun Said's face softened. He looked almost kind. 'Suzanna? She is free to go anywhere she likes, my dear.'

The room stopped spinning and a cold wave of water splashed over me. 'What do you mean?'

Tun Said stood up and pointed to the window on the other side of the room. 'Ask her for yourself.' I wasn't sure what he was referring to. Then at the far end of the field outside the window, I saw a tiny figure in a floppy hat. She wore a loose, flowing blouse over loose baggy trousers; her face bright and beaming.

Chapter 28

Enlightenment

Tun Said pushed open the double doors and a flood of light poured in. It took a moment for my eyes to adjust to the glare. I saw the silhouette of a person standing at the edge of the trees. When the light settled, I noticed the straw of her hat, the lace on the cuff of her blouse.

'Katie,' she said when she saw me. 'What are you doing here?' She tucked the clipboard she was holding under her arm and trotted over to us.

'What are *you* doing here?' I said.

'I'm working on the garden,' she explained. 'Didn't I tell you?'

She beckoned me over and started showing me the plots of land they were working on. There were going to be five rows of herbs and five rows of vegetables. If there was space, they were going to grow mangosteens near the coconut trees.

When I turned around, Tun Said was gone. The smell of roses floated around me and I felt as if I was walking in a field of flowers. Laughter rang over bushes so colourful, they looked like they had been splashed with paint; a mix of maroon, orange, yellow and lime. Beyond these plants, I saw a round pavilion, where a group of woman sat chatting with each other. Some of them wore hats over their hijabs, their scarves draping down strangely from underneath. One woman took a swig from a mineral water bottle. Another fanned herself with a piece of paper. When a bell rang, all of them quickly got up, replacing their hats on their heads.

Suzanna cocked her head at me and asked if I wanted to help. 'Okay,' I said, slowly. She handed me a hoe. The ladies resumed their work, picking up tools that had been left lying on the ground. Suzanna glanced over her shoulder and said she had to go talk to someone. She would be back soon.

So I stood there holding the hoe, not really sure what to do. Most of the women were gathered near the herb garden, digging up weeds and stones. They gave me sidelong looks and whispered among themselves. I don't know if it was my lack of hijab or if it was something else that I was doing wrong.

I think the idea was to get rid of the grass and rubble on the ground, so I jabbed at a pile of rocks nearby. Two white sneakers appeared within my line of vision. Each shoe had a pink squiggle on it. The girl they belonged to had rosebud lips and a rosy pink scarf around her head. Everything about her exuded 'roses'. When she said her name was Rosita, I couldn't help smiling.

'You helping us?' she said.

'I guess so.'

'Use this,' she said. 'It's better.'

I put the other hoe away and took the one she held out to me. She picked up a shovel and started digging the ground.

'Where you from?' she said.

'Australia.'

I paused and glanced at the women on the other side of the field. 'Why do they keep looking here?'

'They're just curious. And they don't speak English that well.'

'You do.'

'Yeah, I'm okay.'

Rosita stood up, her hat flung carelessly against her back. She dug into the ground and chatted away. She did not stop when she paused to wipe her brow or put on her hat. Her mouth broke into a smile, revealing small white teeth.

'You don't talk much, do you?' she said. 'Let me know if I'm talking too much, okay? My mum says I should stop talking so much. She's been saying this since I was like, five. But I have all these things I want to say and it's better to say what's in your head than keep things inside, don't you think?'

I smiled at Rosita. There was just the slightest trace of perspiration on her nose. 'You know, my mum and I haven't spoken to each other for like six months now,' she said. 'If she saw me now, she would be angry anyway. She would think this is a waste of time. When we were young, all she wanted us to do was study. "Mei Gui, you better study hard," she said. "Otherwise you will end up like us.""

'What were they?'

'They sell char kuey teow in SS3. You know the Ming Fatt Restaurant?'

I squinted at Rosita, at the way she spoke the Chinese words. 'Are you Chinese?' I said.

'Yes, didn't you know? I thought I mentioned it.'

Rosita's slender eyes suddenly made sense. She looked a bit like Maggie but with a pink scarf twisted around her head.

'That's why they don't like Rashid,' she said. 'I did everything she wanted. I studied hard, I got a job in a bank, I even bought them a house. But when I told them about Rashid, she acted like I had killed someone.'

I remembered then that Rashid was her fiancé. 'When's the wedding?' I said.

'In December.'

Soon, the sky turned amber, and a man wailed in the forest. His lament grew loud, then soft, then loud again. It took me a moment to realize it was the imam from a nearby mosque. His voice flew through a loud hail over the trees. The women put their tools down and began to disperse.

Suzanna appeared by my side and handed me a glass of lime juice. We went to a stone table at the edge of the garden and surveyed the plots of vegetables. 'Are you really here because you want to be?' I said.

'Yes,' she said, meeting my eyes. 'Is that so hard to believe?'

'I thought they had taken you away,' I blurted, sweat forming in my hands as I recalled the incident. 'There was a raid in the village and they threw out your CDs.'

'I see.' Suzanna was so calm.

'You used to write songs and play music,' I said, trying to keep my voice level. 'Why do you let them stop you from doing what you like? You should be able to—'

'I didn't stop because of them.'

'What?'

Suzanna frowned and pursed her lips together. 'I stopped because the ideas stopped. I was stuck. I was frustrated because I couldn't create anymore.' She shifted her glass and the ice chinked. 'My whole life, I've had this need to create, to let out whatever was burning in my head and I could do it through music. But as time went by, I felt so many things but I couldn't get them out. Every time I started something, it came out wrong and I couldn't finish it. So I stopped everything altogether.'

Suzanna turned to look at me. She had a relieved expression on her face as if she had released a weight she had been bearing for a long time.

'It wasn't because of them?' I said.

'No, in fact, they helped me feel better.'

Suzanna took a deep breath and sighed. 'When I went to Melbourne, I just wanted to get away and start a new life. But when I came back, it felt so strange.'

'Like a foreign place?'

'The opposite actually.'

'The smallest thing would fill me with such joy. Like that tree outside.'

Suzanna pointed to a tree at the edge of the garden. 'Or the smell of salt fish drying on concrete.' She paused and smiled serenely to herself. 'Everyone was so kind and welcoming, it was as if I had come home.'

'You didn't feel that way in Melbourne?'

Suzanna pondered this, the edges of her blue scarf fluttering. 'No,' she said.

The coconut trees swayed in the breeze. A warm wind tickled my elbows.

Suzanna tried to explain the displacement she felt. The times of alienation. The insults that were subtle . . . and not so subtle. When she came back to the village, everyone was so helpful. They brought food over, they welcomed her into their homes. It was like the entire village was her family.

I thought of the Suzanna on the CD cover, the light in her eyes as she gazed up into the spotlight. 'Don't you miss the music?' I said.

Suzanna paused for a moment. 'No, I have my plants.' She said her herbs and plants were a bit like music. There was something extremely satisfying about growing and nurturing plants, and creating herbal blends. You had to draw deep within yourself and tap into a hidden pool of senses. There was often no recipe, she created them by feel. 'It's almost like magic.'

Suzanna looked down at the stone table beside us and studied the tiny specks of quartz in it. 'I'm sorry,' she said. 'I'm so sorry. I know it must have been hard for you.'

'That's okay,' I said, almost automatically, as if she'd bumped into my chair in a restaurant or given me the wrong change. She spoke about wanting a better life for me. She spoke about reconnecting with her faith and finding her place in the world. As the wind swirled around us in a blend of jasmine and thyme, her words did not quite make sense but when I didn't think about it too much, they did. We stood there side-by-side—the same long dark hair, the same silky limbs as the sun broke out of the clouds and filled the sky with gold.

Chapter 29

Hari Raya

After that day, the whole world seemed different. It was as if someone had lifted a veil off my face. Suzanna's house, which I thought quaint before, took on an even more intriguing quality. I noticed things I hadn't before. Like the Arabic words embroidered in golden thread. Or the way the sun shone through the gossamer curtains and created specks of light on the floor.

One day, I had gone over and was having a cup of tea in Suzanna's kitchen when she said, 'Can you wait for a while? I need to do something.' She slipped into a nearby room, leaving the door ajar. She donned a white robe and slid a white poncho over her head. She rolled out a little Persian rug and stepped onto it. She bent down, she stood up, bent down, and stood up again. A gentle glow spread in the room and the hairs at the back of my neck tingled. It's hard to explain—it was a bit like St Patrick's Cathedral on Christmas Eve, when the choir sang 'Ave Maria'.

'Sorry,' said Suzanna, coming into the kitchen. 'It was *Asar*.' A wispy grey hijab was wrapped around her head in a way I'd never seen before. The scarf swirled up high with the soft material falling gently over her back.

'Are you going somewhere?' I said.

'We both are.'

She squinted at the hat rack near the door and grabbed a long silky scarf. 'You can use my *selendang*.' She placed the cloth over my head. The light material kissed my cheek and grazed the edge of my elbow. Suzanna draped the end of the scarf over my left shoulder and said, 'There'. Just before we left, I stole a glance at myself in the hallway mirror. I looked like me—with a scarf on my head.

* * *

As we walked down the driveway, my phone rang. It was Maggie, 'Hey,' she said, brightly. 'Where are you?'

'Oh, I'm out.'

'I thought you were studying at Starbucks. Aren't you at the Starbucks in Mid Valley?' My mind began to race. I had told them that I'd be there yesterday . . .

'We came over to say hi but I don't see you. You still at the mall?'

My words faltered. 'No . . . I had to go run an errand.'

'Oh, I see.' A motorbike blared past.

'What is that sound?' exclaimed Maggie. 'Where are you?' Some Malay music rang in the air. I prayed for it to disappear, but it only got louder.

'Are you outdoors?' said Maggie.

'Yeah, I'm walking on the road. I have to go soon. I'll see you back at the house? If you're in.'

'You won't join us for dinner?'

I gave Suzanna a quick glance. 'Er, no, it's okay. You go on ahead.'

When I hung up, my heart was pounding. Suzanna did not ask me who it was. We kept on walking along the road lined with coconut trees. She smiled and told me it was the month of Ramadan. How it was a holy month and people fasted from dawn to dusk. At sundown, everyone gathered to eat together. We arrived at a house with a big marquee in front. Its white sails extended from the porch to the street. Tables filled up the driveway, each covered with a white tablecloth.

A lady waved at us from the terrace. Suzanna waved back. We walked up to her and Suzanna introduced me to Maimunah. She wore a midnight blue kebaya which hugged every curve of her body. When she shook my hand, her eyelashes curled up, thick with mascara. If Suzanna looked stylish, Maimunah looked royal; her blouse glittering with silver thread, gold dust shining on her cheeks.

I fiddled with the scarf Suzanna had lent me. I had to keep flipping the end over my shoulder. When I looked up, I saw a small Malay man standing on the front steps of the house greeting guests. It took me a second to recognize Tun Said in his shimmery cream top. A long line of people snaked up the steps to shake hands with him. Everyone was dressed in clothes that seemed to shimmer in the street light: bright pinks, silvery blues, shiny maroon. I felt slightly underdressed in my Cotton On blouse, but the selendang kind of made up for it with its sequinned trim.

I watched the way Maimunah spoke to people. Suzanna said she was a dancer, and I could see it in the way she moved. She was neither slender nor slim and was quite chunky, really, but when she walked, she gave the illusion of ultimate grace. Her hips swung from side to side, her shoulders swayed. When she shook hands with people, she extended her hands out so gracefully, it looked like part of a dance. I tried to memorize her moves: unfolding her hands out and bringing them in. She was wearing a selendang like me, but it never fell off, staying magically attached to her shoulders at all times.

Suzanna left me to talk to some friends of hers in the driveway. I went into the house to look for the bathroom. The chandelier twinkled overhead, lighting up Persian carpets and a marble floor.

I asked someone where the bathroom was and they pointed me to a door near the staircase. I went inside and found myself in a study of sorts. A piano stood in the corner and bookshelves lined the wall. 'Hello,' said a voice. 'Thanks for coming.' Tun Said stood by a desk in the shadows.

'Oh, hi,' I said. 'I didn't see you there. I was looking for the bathroom.'

'It's over there.' He pointed towards a door outlined by light. 'I think someone is inside.'

'Oh, okay.'

Tun Said opened a drawer and rummaged through it. He appeared to be looking for something. I studied the pictures on the wall. 'Is that you?' I said, pointing at a photo of a man in a robe.

'No, that's my father.'

The man in the black-and-white photo wore a white Haji's hat and was looking straight at the camera. The next picture featured the same guy receiving a medal from a sultan or king. 'Was he a politician too?' I said.

'Yes, Minister of Rural Development.'

'What is he doing now?'

'He's passed on.'

'Sorry to hear.'

'He was a great leader. He had big dreams for the country. Some people even thought he would be the next Prime Minister. But he ended up in jail—that's where he died. That's democracy for you.'

'I see.' I kept quiet. This story sounded loaded with politics and I was not keen on engaging in another debate. A clock ticked on the side table and the sound echoed through the room. Someone flushed the toilet and the door at the side opened.

* * *

When I went back outside, Suzanna was nowhere to be found. The marquee blinked with fairy lights and strings of *ketupat*. The sound of music drew me towards the back of the house. I followed the tinkles down a dimly lit path. When I passed a large hibiscus bush, I stopped. 'Nasa?' I said. 'Is that you?'

'Hi!' said Nasa. He slunk out from the shadows. The glow from the oil lamps illuminated his spiky hair, slicker and brighter— his party look, perhaps.

'What are you doing here?' I said. 'You know Tun Said?'

Nasa chuckled. 'Everyone knows Tun Said. And you?'

'I'm here with Suzanna.' I peered into the bushes. 'What's in there?' I could make out some kind of hut or shed. 'Are they playing music there?'

'Oh, no, no, there is nothing there,' said Nasa hurriedly. 'It's all muddy. I think the music's there,' he said, pointing towards the light. When I turned back to look at him, he smiled again and nodded. 'It was nice seeing you,' he said. 'But I have to go.'

He clutched his satchel. Nasa seemed to be holding it excessively tightly as if he were afraid his things would fall out.

'Have you been here long?' I asked.

'No, not too long,' he said, his words coming out clipped and fast. 'But I have to get back to work.' I remembered then that Nasa worked at a music store in one of the malls.

'It was nice seeing you,' I said.

'Yes, bye!' said Nasa, already starting to walk away. He strode off, clasping his bag and hurrying into the darkness. I'd hoped he would hang around a bit longer. It was nice to see a familiar face. Xylophone chimes tinkled in the back garden and I padded after the sounds.

I saw twelve people sitting cross-legged on a stage, each one with a kind of gong in front of them. A lady in a very pretty kebaya was singing in Malay. 'Have you seen *gamelan* before?' said Suzanna, suddenly appearing beside me. I shook my head.

'I love it,' she said. 'It is so basic but when everyone plays together, it is so powerful.'

The lead player began to escalate into a faster beat, and the others followed, as if trying to catch up with him. 'This song is about rain,' whispered Suzanna. I didn't even need to understand the words. I imagined rain drops falling, each one dancing to a different tune and I recalled that day at the shack with Justin. We sat through a few more songs, each one different from the rest. A love song, a fighting song, a song that made you soar into the air. Suzanna grabbed her bag. 'I'll see you in a bit,' she said.

'Where are you going?'

'Oh, it's time for *Terawih* prayers.' She pointed at a tent on the other side of the garden.

'What's that?'

'Just some prayers for Ramadan.'

'Can I come?'

Suzanna glanced at the trees. 'No . . .'

'Why not?'

She glanced at the trees again.

'Is it because I'm not Muslim?'

'Yes,' she said softly. 'But I won't be long. You carry on watching.'

I noticed the garden had gone quiet. There were only a few people milling about. Most of them were probably in the tent. To say light was coming out from it would not be precisely correct. It was more like an essence; like Suzanna's house this afternoon, when she was praying.

Suzanna stood up and the clouds above me gushed in slow motion like they were telling me something. Words bubbled out of me before I fully knew what they were. 'How do I learn more about it?' I said. 'I want to know more.'

Suzanna scoffed. 'You don't have to,' she said with a smile.

'I want to,' I said.

'Don't be silly, it's just a small ceremony. I will be out soon.'

A trampled hibiscus lay on the grass. Its petals crushed with dew. 'I've been thinking about this for a while,' I told her. 'Remember you said it just hit you one day when you came back? I feel it too. I need to know more to understand if it's the right thing for me.'

Suzanna frowned at the trees hovering at the edge of the garden. 'You want to go for classes?'

'Yes, classes' I exclaimed like I'd struck gold. She looked at me with a slight frown. 'Okay,' she said, studying my face. She examined my eyes. She examined my mouth. She looked like she was studying everything there was to see about me. 'Okay,' she said again, breaking into a smile.

Chapter 30

Cracks

Some days, I would go out with Maggie and Roy. Others (actually, most others), I would go to see Suzanna. Everyone thought I was busy at Starbucks studying for the scholarship exams (which I did, a few times) so they left me to my own devices. Pa? Pa was Pa. Absent and busy as usual. We went to church and dinner with Tua Ee a couple of times, but that was pretty much it.

As the days went by, I began to see bits of myself in Suzanna. She would arrange all her cups in the cupboard the same way, with each cup two inches apart. If a book in a stack was sticking out, she pushed it back into place. When she brought in her tea towels from the clothesline, she folded them according to colour. The reds and pinks would go together, followed by the different shades of green.

She was actually quite reserved and could go hours without speaking. Quite often, she would be jotting things down in a jade-green notebook. Once, I saw her doing this while I was doing my homework and I said, 'What's that?'

'Nothing,' she said, quickly putting the notebook away.

She carried it with her all the time, in her apron pocket or in a sling pouch strapped across her body. Whenever she thought of something, she would stop and write in it, as if she were recording passing ideas.

I can't pinpoint the exact time things started to get odd but it must have been around the day she asked me to collect some herbs for her from the garden. I put a basket of mint and a basket of *pegaga* beside her on the table. She looked up at me.

'What are you doing?' Her eyes turned dark. The wings of her eyeliner looked even more pronounced as she examined the leaves in front of her.

'You asked me to get these just now.'

She frowned at me.

Did I get it wrong? That was pegaga, right? I did not know the English word for it, but Suzanna had shown me which they were.

'Why do I need pegaga?' she said. 'I asked for ulam leaves.'

'No, you asked for pegaga—for the hand ointment.'

'Hand ointment?' she looked at me like I had just insulted her. 'If it's for hand ointment, I need more than that! I need kaffir lime as well. You should know that, right?' Suzanna glared at the two baskets on the table. She looked very cross about the whole matter.

'I'll get the kaffir lime,' I mumbled.

She barely acknowledged my words. She inspected the mint and turned back to her notebook, her forehead all furrowed up. I knew something was bothering her. We remained quiet for the next hour or so. She gazed out the window, a glazed look in her eyes. It reminded me of Riana. Had nothing really happened at Sungai Besi? It crossed my mind that maybe she *had* been rehabilitated.

* * *

Later that day, we went to Mak Minah's Kedai Runcit to get some groceries. Suzanna needed to drop something off at the post office so she said she would meet me back at the shop. Mak Minah always had a smile for me when I came in. She would speak to me in broken English and sneak me extra goodies like fruit or lollies, whenever she could. She seemed thrilled to be able to share stuff with me as if I was some strange new breed of person she was tasked to educate.

That day, I spotted her in the sauce aisle, loading up cans of sardines onto a shelf. Her floral baju kurung looked as fresh as the carnations on her counter. 'Hallo,' she called out, flashing me a row of crooked teeth. 'Selamat pagi!'

'Selamat pagi,' I replied, carefully enunciating my words.

She placed the last can on the shelf and got up from the floor. 'Today, we have good rambutan,' she said. 'You like rambutan?'

'What is that?' I said.

She pointed to a bunch of hairy red things on the table.

'Is that a fruit?' I said. She nodded. She peeled one off the branch and gave it to me, this hairy red fruit, smaller than a tomato. I was about to take a bite when she stopped me. 'No, no, no,' bustled Mak Minah. 'You open.'

She took a rambutan in her hand and twisted the skin off to reveal a small white ball inside, shiny and smooth like an egg. I popped it into my mouth—so sweet and delicious! Then I chomped onto something hard. Mak Minah laughed, revealing a couple of black fillings at the back of her mouth. 'Got seed.' She spat out the seed from the rambutan she was eating into her hand and threw it into the bin.

'You buy?' she said.

I grabbed a bunch of rambutans and a can of coconut milk. Then I went outside to wait for Suzanna. I was early. I reckoned it would be another five minutes before she came. I took out my phone and sent Dessi a picture of the rambutan.

Dessi   : Omg what's that?
Me   : It's a rambutan, a fruit.
Dessi   : Looks like a sea urchin.

I showed her a picture of the juicy flesh inside and told her it was really delicious. I tried to think of a similar fruit in Australia but I couldn't. She sent me back a shot of the Berwick Swimming Centre, a row of gum trees in front of it. I could tell she was at our usual bus stop.

Me   : **Just finished school?**
Dessi   : **Yup, you're missing some fine weather here.**

She showed me another picture and I could see rain pouring down, puddles of water on the ground.

Me   : **You headed to the library?**
Dessi   : **Nope, I'm going to the tennis centre.**
Me   : **You're playing tennis?**
Dessi   : **Haha yup. Just started classes.**
Me   : **In this rain?**
Dessi   : **Well, it's supposed to stop.**
Me   : **You believe the weather forecast?**

I looked up from my phone. Suzanna had still not arrived. Two school girls walked by, eating ice-cream potong. Their red bean lollies glistened in the sun as they chatted away melodiously. If I concentrated, I could recognize some of the words they used and if I concentrated even harder, I could even understand what they were saying.

I checked my phone but there was no reply from Dessi, so I put it away. Across the road, a street vendor was frying goreng pisang. Sizzling sounds filled the air as he dipped the wired ladle into the oil. Melbourne seemed far away but I was happy to be exactly where I was.

As the vendor pulled out a bunch of banana fritters, I saw a familiar shape in the distance. Suzanna walked across the street in her grey hijab. Something about the way she walked made me feel that something was not right. She looked like she wanted to be invisible, clutching her bag tightly. She tiptoed down the street towards me but when she reached the next junction, she turned left.

I walked briskly towards her and saw her standing further down the street. She stood in front of the butcher shop, peering across the road, as if waiting for something. She kept looking at her phone and looking up again. I waited a few minutes but no one came. 'Suzanna?' I said, as I approached her.

'Why are you so late?' she grumbled.

'I'm not late. I thought we were meeting back at the convenience store.'

'No, I said the butcher. That is halfway. Why would I go all the way back to the store?'

Suzanna hitched up her bag and began marching down the road. What was she hiding? Had she been planning to meet someone? Throughout the way, Suzanna did not say a word. I trudged two steps behind her, trying to keep up. When we reached a junction, we waited to cross the road. A motorbike trundled past. Suzanna wiped her eyes with a knuckle. When she moved her hand away, I saw a tear glimmering on her cheek.

Chapter 31

Pa Returns

Pa had finally come back from his Ipoh business trip. I still hadn't had a chance to talk to him about Suzanna. It's not like he would have brought it up anyway. He was one of those people who would ignore problems until they disappeared. If you waited long enough, it would go away, wouldn't it? That's how he was whenever we argued about things. He never apologized or gave concrete solutions. He would just make me a glass of Milo or ask about school one day and whatever we'd disagreed about would disappear—but it never really disappeared, it was just brushed under the carpet. If you looked at that carpet now, it would look like a mountain.

The next morning at Tua Ee's house, I found him in the kitchen. He was dousing a piece of roti in a pool of curry. He gave no indication that the last time we spoke, we were discussing the enormous lie that was my life, or that he had promised to tell me everything the next time we met. 'No work today?' I asked.

'No, not really.'

'How can you eat that so early?' I said.

'Why not? I used to have this for breakfast all the time.'

All the time. In Melbourne, I'd only seen him have toast or Weet-bix. I went to the larder and opened it. I wasn't even sure what I was looking for. I stared at the Nescafe and Milo cans inside then I closed the larder door. 'How have you been?' Pa said. 'Sorry I have been so busy. Have you been bored? I heard you've been hanging out with Roy and Maggie.'

'Yeah.' To be honest, I hung out with Suzanna most of the time. 'I've also been busy with schoolwork,' I added. 'Holiday classes have started.'

'Oh yes, I've been meaning to ask you,' Pa said. 'Do you want to go back to Melbourne earlier? I don't want you to miss so many classes.'

Pa's words hit me like a bomb, 'It's okay,' I gushed. 'Mr. Stockton said I'm fine working remotely. In fact, I'm ahead of my work. I brought all my books with me.'

'No really, you can go back first, and I'll come in a few weeks.'

I narrowed my eyes at Pa. 'What do you need to do?'

'I have a few more things to tie up with the lawyers.'

'Really?' I glanced at the window and turned back to him.

'Yes, also, there is an election coming,' Pa said with a frown. 'I heard things might get a bit messy here. I don't want you to—'

'Is this because of Suzanna?' I cried.

'What?'

'Are you trying to keep me away from her?'

'Of course not, I just thought—'

'I saw you at her house the other day,' I said, my heart pounding. I kept my gaze fixed, suddenly feeling more courageous. In fact, maybe it wasn't courage, more like anger, a hot sticky streak that was zipping up my chest. 'What were you doing there?'

Pa faltered. 'I needed to talk to her about something.'

'Really? How often have you been going?'

He fumbled again. 'That was the first time.'

I watched Pa frown at his half-eaten drumstick. I was not letting him go this time. I imagined I had caught him in a silver lasso and I would not let go until he spoke. He gave the chicken a prod and put the fork down.

'I know you have been going there,' I said. 'Why did you have to lie?'

'I didn't lie,' he said quietly. 'I just went there that one time.'

'Not about seeing her. About everything.' I thought of all those years he had said nothing to me, letting the lie grow bigger and bigger. What had happened really, what were they keeping me from me? Did something happen to make her leave? And then it hit me like a big fat bomb on my head. 'Were you seeing someone else?' I said.

'Of course not.' Pa scoffed. 'Sometimes things just don't work out.'

'So why didn't you just tell me the truth?'

Pa let out a big sigh. 'I didn't want you to be upset.'

'And telling me she was dead was better?'

Pa glanced at his phone. 'Oh, Diana said she can pick you up from the airport,' he said breezily, 'Can we make it Friday?' There he went again, avoiding things. I'd had enough of this. He didn't want to talk and I couldn't be bothered either. I didn't need to get answers from him anymore, I could get them from someone else.

'Where are you going?' Pa said. 'We've got church.'

'I'm not going.'

'Why?'

'I need to go out.' Maybe he said, 'Where?' 'Who are you seeing?' Or even, 'I'm sorry, let's talk some more', but I didn't hear any of it. I grabbed my bag and dashed out the door. I kept running—past the street filled with potholes and the broken stop sign—until I saw the tall grey walls of the LRT (Light Rail Transit) station.

Chapter 32

Justin Again

Rosita and I were walking back from religious classes. We had gone a few times already. We took an old logging track that cut through the forest, the ground still wet from last night's rain. As I followed the trail of Rosita's sneakers—striped prints on red clay—I thought about what the *ustaz* had just spoken to us about.

'Is the FM18 really that bad?' I said aloud. Rosita stopped and stared at me wide-eyed. 'It's black metal,' she replied. 'Didn't you hear what Ustaz said? It's . . . *Satan's music.*' She whispered the last two words as if saying them might conjure up demons in the sunshine. It was hard to imagine anything supernatural under this glare.

'It's also on the same day as the Conversion Ceremony,' said Rosita. 'And at the same place.'

'At Dataran Merdeka?'

'Yep.' No wonder Tun Said was against it. It would be weird to have these two things happening at the same time. I pictured a Muslim ceremony on one side and the very kind of concert they were against on the other.

Further down the path, a man was pushing his bicycle towards us, wobbling slightly with the weight of the coconuts in his basket. I moved aside to let him pass. When I jumped back, I found myself face to face with a guy who had come out of nowhere. The sun shone from behind, making him a tall black shape.

'Hey,' said Justin.

'Hey,' I said.

'Can we talk?' His eyes were fixed on me. I'd never seen him look so serious before. I turned to Rosita and told her to go ahead. 'I'll meet you at the hall.'

'You sure?'

'Yes, save me a seat.'

Justin and I stood on the path staring at each other. 'What's going on?' he asked. His face was fresh and luminous, as if he'd just stepped out of the shower. A farmer in an adjacent field stopped to peer at us. 'Let's go over there.' Justin pointed towards some trees.

We trod down a narrower path, the sound of running water filling up the silence between us. Leaves crunched under our feet, insects chirped from beneath the soil. When we reached the shade of a fern, Justin stopped. 'So, what happened?'

'What do you mean?'

'What happened at the rehabilitation centre?'

'It's all good,' I said. 'I found my mum.'

'And?'

'And she's fine,' I replied, blinking up at him.

A chicken crowed from the back of a house. It strutted across the yard, sticking its neck out here and there. 'Why haven't you been replying to my messages?' Justin said.

'I have . . . I said I got home okay.'

Justin tilted his head and studied my face. 'Katie, that was over a week ago.'

The wind gushed in my ears. Had it been that long? How had the time passed by so quickly? Justin continued drilling his eyes into mine. 'What happened?' he said. 'Why are you dressed like this?' The wind whipped up the edges of the headscarf Suzanna had given to me.

'What's wrong?' I said, looking down at my outfit. 'Everyone wears this.'

Justin turned away, his collarbone gleaming above his T-shirt.

'Why do you care anyway?' I said, remembering how he had pulled away at the teh tarik stall. He shoved his hands into his pocket. 'You said you would message me when you got back home,' he muttered. 'I had to call you three times before you messaged back. And then you never answered any of my calls.'

That was true. I had a vague recollection of the calls coming in. 'I've just been busy,' I mumbled.

'I kept wondering, why hasn't she called? What is she doing?' Justin rubbed his forehead. 'You think I like doing this?'

I swallowed. Why was he acting like this? 'Are you angry with me?' I said.

Tiny creatures pattered in the undergrowth. Justin glanced away, then he turned back. 'Everyone is worried about you,' he said.

'What do you mean, everyone?'

'Well, Nasa said he bumped into you over Hari Raya.' He paused. 'And . . . I'm worried too.'

I let out a small laugh. 'Are you like this with everyone? People might get the wrong idea.'

Justin stared at me like he was wrestling with something. I felt my heart race. The sounds of running water grew louder.

'I'm just . . .' he faltered, struggling with his words. 'I just . . .' He frowned so adorably I felt like taking his hand. Was it what I had imagined? What I had hoped?

'Why didn't you say anything before?' I whispered.

Justin exhaled heavily then he frowned again. 'I wanted to,' he stammered. 'But . . . don't you know who your father is?'

My blood began to boil. 'What, because he's Chinese?' I said, my voice hard. 'I thought you didn't care about things like that.'

'I don't!' exclaimed Justin. 'But . . .' Again, he faltered.

I knew it. It was like Suzanna and Pa all over again.

'Come on,' he said, taking my wrist. 'Let's talk about this later. I'll give you a lift back.'

'No.'

Justin let go. 'Why?'

'I told you, I need to go to a meeting.'

His eyes turned dark. 'Katie,' he said. 'You don't know these people, you don't know what they're like.'

'And you do?'

'Yes.'

A heat began to rise in my chest. Who was he to tell me what to do? He was the one who was afraid to do anything. 'You don't care about anything, do you?' I retorted. 'You always don't want to be involved. FM18? No, I'm not interested. Wira group? No, I'm not with them. Well, I'm not like you. I've found my mum and I'm not going to give up on that.'

Justin let out a sigh. Voices. Footsteps. Wira soldiers patrolling in the distance. 'I've decided,' I said firmly, 'so stop trying to stop me.' I scampered up the hill but halfway up, I tripped over a rock and stumbled. Darn, I had hoped to make a cool exit. I steadied myself and a voice said, 'Are you okay?' Two Wira soldiers peered at me through the bushes.

'This guy bothering you?' One of them pointed at Justin, who stood in the grove below, glowering. His very presence set off so many prickles in my body, and I felt like the whole world was against me. I gritted my teeth and said, 'Yes, he is'.

Chapter 33

Wira Mission

When I got to the hall, the event had already started. I spotted Rosita's pink scarf among the sea of black heads. I slid into the empty seat beside her and turned my attention to the stage. One of the senior Wira people was speaking. I barely listened to what he said as he droned on in Malay. I scanned the audience and spotted Nasa a few rows away. He sat on the last chair at the end, his hands in his lap. I didn't know he was into these things. I thought he was a bit like Justin. But he seemed rather attentive—smiled at jokes and clapped when everyone clapped.

I checked my phone but there was no word from Justin. There was a message from Roy.

Roy : Project at 11 a.m. today. See you at the school?

I forgot I had promised him I would go!

Me : Sorry, something came up . . . I'll go next time.

Before I could write anything more, a round of applause rang through the room. The lady beside me cast me a sharp look and I quickly put my phone away. Tun Said stood behind the lectern, looking like a Muslim priest in his long, white robe and his perfectly trimmed moustache. *'Bismillah-ir-Rahman-ir-Rahim. . .'* he chanted. Everyone bowed their heads and cupped their hands together. After the prayer ended, they said, 'Amin', rubbing both hands over their faces.

'Amin,' said Rosita. 'Amin,' I said, doing the same. I loved this part of the prayer, wiping my hands over my face as if I was cleaning it and coming out anew. I took a deep breath and took in Tun Said's speech as he outlined the progress of his campaign. He spoke in Malay but it was different from the other guy. I didn't have to understand the words to make me want to listen. A PowerPoint slide behind him flashed with the number of seats he had in Lembah Pantai, then along came pictures of a mosque and people in Malay clothing cheering on a street. Tun Said gestured to the crowd, pinching his fingers together as he emphasized each point. He had this ability to make you believe whatever he said.

'The sky is red.'

'Cats hate fish.'

'The Martians are coming.'

I noticed how his words rose and fell, the way only a person who didn't know the language could notice. Tun Said scanned the sea of heads, using the silence as much as his voice. When the crowd could no longer contain their excitement, he delivered his concluding thoughts. The colour of his face deepened and a vein pulsed at his neck. He ended with a final cry—*Hidup Melayu!*—and the crowd roared. I, too, stood up amidst the thundering chairs, and clapped my hands.

* * *

After the gathering, a bunch of us went to the Lembah Pantai community hall to get it ready for Tun Said's next rally. Rosita and I lugged two boxes towards the foyer, the others headed to the nearby hill to clear the flags. 'What did you think of the speech?' said Rosita.

'Is he trying to build some kind of Islamic country?'

'Yes, wouldn't it be great if the whole country accepted Islam? We could be such a great nation.'

'Even the non-Malays?'

'Yes, why not? Islam doesn't discriminate, anyone can embrace the religion.'

I put down my bucket and took out the first poster inside. I unrolled the glossy paper to reveal a picture of Tun Said in his Haji's hat. There was a Che Guevara look about him as he gazed out into the distance. I could only guess what he saw. A city of turrets? A nation of Muslims? I imagined the world Suzanna often spoke about. A community so caring and peaceful, you could feel their warmth as you walked down the street. A family that ate, prayed and planted together, coconut trees swaying in the breeze.

I pasted that poster and picked up another. As I unrolled the paper, I heard tyres crunch on the asphalt. Three motorbikes pulled up and stopped in front of the foyer. They were not huge bikes like Harley Davidsons, they were small, scrawny, shiny and dark like demon horses. Were these the Mat Rempit Tua Teow had spoken about? One of the guys got off and waved at Rosita. He had a small weaselly head and sallow brown skin. Everything about him resembled some sort of marsupial. Rosita put down a roll of cello tape and went over to meet him.

As I turned to pick up another poster, I could feel the guy's shifty eyes crawling over me. Rosita came striding back. 'Who was that?' I asked.

'Firhad. Do you know him?'

I shook my head.

'You might have seen him in the village. He and his boys are always wandering around.'

I reached for my scissors. 'Does he know me?'

'Everyone knows you,' she said, smiling.

The motorbikes lay at the end of the car park, hidden by the trees. The four guys stood in a circle talking. One had his hands in his pockets, the other stretched out his arms and yawned. The third picked up a metal pipe and began whacking something on the ground. He kept hitting it until it broke into splinters, the whole affair inducing a round of laughter. Firhad swatted him on the back of his head and made his way into the trees.

I saw him a minute later, weaving through the tall grasses. He waded one way and then another. He finally settled on a small raised clearing. He stood right in the centre and lifted a bunch of leaves above his head. I thought he was clearing out some weeds but then smoke began to rise as he swayed the bunch from side to side.

'What is he doing?' I said, gesturing to the hill.

'Some ritual,' replied Rosita.

'For what?'

'For good luck. They always do that before a rally.'

Firhad raised the leaf stack up and down, then up and down again. He let go of the last burning leaf and it sank to the ground. I wondered what lay at his feet. A charm like in Suzanna's house the other day? What other spells had he cast?

Towards his right, I noticed some movement along the slope. Alek and Din bobbed up and down, pulling out flags as they went along. I couldn't help but think of Roy and planting the flags with him in the Lake Gardens two weeks ago. *Roy!* I pulled out my phone and saw that he had messaged.

Roy   : We'll be going to Lembah Pantai at about 5 p.m. It's not far from us. Let me know if you can come.

The moment I read the location, my heart began to race. Was Roy coming here? I whipped my head up and scanned the area. I checked the time—5.05 p.m. No, maybe it wouldn't be here. I continued pasting the posters and as I was putting the last one up, I heard a car creak into the side car park. I say 'creak' because that's what it sounded like. The tyres crept up the road and rolled into the parking area near me. Something white glinted behind the hedge.

Through a crack in the branches, I saw an ivory-coloured Charade. I knew who they were even before the doors opened. Maggie stepped out in her signature bob. Two other guys whom I didn't recognize, jumped out. When they turned towards me, I quickly hid behind a pole.

I peeped out again and saw Roy slip out of the driver's seat and head straight for the boot. He moved like clockwork, pulling out a torch, a duffel bag and a basket I knew was filled with flags.

'Hey,' said Rosita from the end of the corridor. 'Are you finished?'

'Almost,' I said, picking up a flag line.

It was that semi-dark time between evening and night. The streetlights were on but the day was still too bright for them to take effect. Roy scanned the car park and saw nothing except for a big green hedge. He did not see our car in the higher car park or Firhad's motorbike hidden in the trees.

Doors slammed, the boot opened again. All these noises sounded extra loud in the evening air. There was a faint smell of burning. 'Hey,' said Rosita, coming up to me. 'You done?'

I flinched, gripping the string of flags in my hand. 'Just got to hang this,' I said. 'Why don't you go ahead first?' I fiddled with a knot and ignored my racing heart.

Rosita said she would pack up first. 'I'll see you at the car.'

'Okay,' I replied in an upbeat tone.

Maggie's voice rang through the air, the way it did at Tua Ee's house when she came back from school. I willed her to keep quiet but she kept talking. Rosita strode towards the main car park. I couldn't see Firhad or any of the other guys. Perhaps they were already making their way down the hill, metal pipes in hand.

Rosita leaned against the side of the car, tapping her fingers on the door. Roy and the others were silent again. They could take care of themselves. Then one of Roy's friend's laughed and the sound pierced the air like a horn. A medley of images filled my mind: Roy's football jersey hanging on the washing line that morning; Maggie raving about this Chinese pop star she liked; the both of them laughing at me eating nasi lemak with a spoon. The answer was clear. I put down my bucket and ran towards the hedge.

Chapter 34

Leak

I was happily eating my mee hoon goreng in the Wira canteen, about to dig into a hard-boiled egg, when this girl came up and stood in front of me. She was wearing jeans and a pretty sky-blue hijab made from a material so light and soft, the sunlight sifted through it like a ballerina's skirt. She stood there like some kind of dancer herself, slender and sleight, as if waiting for me to do something. Did I know her?

'Hi,' she said but it sounded more like 'Hng'. I remembered her then. She was Lisa, the girl who didn't have a tongue. Rumour had it that they cut it off because she had lied about something. I was never 100 per cent sure about these things—people talked a lot in the village. There were stories about spirits who lived in the trees and a bridge you were not supposed to cross because a baby ghost lived under it.

Lisa slid a piece of paper towards me. It was a white piece of paper folded into half. 'Tun Said wants to see you,' it said.

'Oh,' I said, putting my fork down. 'Do you know why?' She shook her head. Suddenly, I no longer felt like eating the egg. I took a sip of water and wiped my mouth. I folded my serviette and placed it onto the plate.

* * *

His door was slightly ajar. It felt like a principal's office. You didn't quite know what was inside but you had a feeling it could be unpleasant. For some reason, I tasted something like mint in my mouth, mint and metal, like at a dentist's. I gave a small knock and the door swung open. 'Morning,' I said. 'You wanted to see me?'

'Hello,' he said, eyes steely. 'Have a seat.' He rattled off light commentaries—how was I finding the weather, how was the food in the canteen. His words hummed into the air. It had been a while since I'd been in someone's 'office'. All the psychologists seemed to have a similar setup. Plant. Picture. A shelf filled with things.

Tun Said's office carried the same vibe—I half-expected a box there to hold games like Hungry Hippo or that Pirate one all the therapists seemed to love.

'You like military history?' said Tun Said.

'What?'

He gestured to the shelf and I noticed the rows of books on it: *Sun Tzu: The Art of War*, *Stalingrad*, *The Guns of August*.

'No, not really,' I replied. 'Do you?'

'Yes,' he said, eyes aglow. 'You can learn a lot about life from it.'

Now that he mentioned it, there was a military gait about him. He was not tall but carried his body in a way that made him look it. Every part of his person was in a perfect position from the lay of his fringe to the ruby ring on his finger. He observed me now as if trying to extract something from my mind.

'How are you finding the religious education classes?' he asked.

I hesitated. Was this a test? 'They're okay,' I mumbled before meeting his eyes.

He paused, tilting his head so deliberately I thought I heard it creak.

'To be honest,' he said. 'I didn't think you would convert. It must be quite different from what you're used to.'

'It's not that different, actually. I found lots of similarities. The names of the Prophets, the stories. It's like we are all using the same source of knowledge. I like how it's simpler though, it just feels right.'

Tun Said narrowed his eyes as if he was saying, 'Is that really why you're doing it?' He picked up a strange object from his table, a paper weight perhaps—it had sharp spikes and was made of metal—and began to twirl it through his fingers. Someone said the other day that Tun Said didn't feel pain; I wondered if that was true.

The sun shone through the window and made shadows of everything. The photo. The pen cup. A glass bottle. Tun Said continued twirling the spiky ball and then he stopped. His whole aura changed as if light had come into the room or a curtain had lifted. 'So, how did things go at Lembah Pantai yesterday?'

My heart skipped a beat. 'Okay,' I replied smoothly. 'We managed to put all the posters up.'

'That's good, that's good.' He tilted his head to the side and sat up straighter. 'I noticed something strange is going on,' he muttered. 'I think someone has been talking to the Mentari people.'

'What do you mean?' I could feel sweat forming on my palms.

'Some people from the Mentari group went to the Lembah Pantai community hall yesterday. But then they suddenly left. Do you know why?'

'I don't know.' My voice sounded strangled.

'Yes, it's strange, isn't it?' Tun Said's gaze stayed on me. 'Firhad said he saw them drive in. I think they were flag planters but then they suddenly packed up and left. It's as if someone warned them at the last minute.'

I did not know what to do. Tun Said continued to look at me like he could see inside my brain. *Should I tell him the truth?*

I thought of Lisa. Her frail shape in the sun as she went about her day in groans and grunts. 'Maybe they had a call at the last minute.' I said. My voice sounded weak and shallow.

'Yes, maybe.' Tun Said squinted his eyes and continued frowning at the table. Then he clicked his tongue and said, 'Oh, yes, I called you over because I seem to be missing something.'

'What is it?'

'A notebook. It's got some important information inside. I thought you might have seen it as it was in the study when I bumped into you the other night.' I recalled that night, the Ramadan dinner. 'It's just a small notebook, about this big.' He made the size of a bar of chocolate with his hands. 'Do you have any idea where it could be?'

'No.' I honestly didn't but Tun Said kept looking at me as if he was clutching me by the collar. This time, I was brave enough to meet his eyes. He stared at me, I stared at him. Then he clicked his tongue again. It was a strange sound, like a cluck in his throat. I noticed he did this when he was thinking or had decided on something. 'So you really haven't seen it?'

I shook my head.

'Not even in Suzanna's house?'

Suzanna. I thought of that book she carried with her everywhere she went. Is that what he was looking for? The thoughts came tumbling in: the way she was always skulking around or jumping at things; scribbling things in the corner. Was she the one leaking information? I cleared my throat. 'No, I haven't seen it.' Tun Said continued staring, his moustache trimmed so perfectly, it seemed that anything else in the world out of alignment was committing a crime.

My mind continued to flash with memories of Suzanna wandering off to different places without telling me. Waiting for someone at a street corner or doubling back saying she'd forgotten something. What was she hiding? Whose side was she on? 'I guess it will turn up somewhere,' Tun Said concluded.

Just like that, he broke into a smile. A small breeze flit into the room, fluttering the leaf of a plant. 'There is one more thing.' Tun Said crossed his fingers together and leaned forward. He said he had a job for me. Yes, I would be the best person for it. He told me about it, making it sound really casual and matter-of-fact, like a trip to the supermarket. When he finished speaking, I unclenched my hands.

'You think you can do that?' he said.

'Sure.'

He leaned back in his seat, his moustache lifting ever so slightly. For the first time that day, he looked pleased as if he'd completed a job. He squeezed the paper weight in his hand and I imagined the spikes piercing through his skin. There was a soft smile on his face as if he was thinking about a rabbit or small hamster. 'I'll see you then,' I said. When I got up, I wiped my hands on my trousers. They were drenched.

Chapter 35

Mentari Rally

My job was to go to the Mentari rally and find out anything I could about Tony Ong—a leader recently released from jail who had yet to make a public appearance. Word was that he was going to hold this meeting of leaders soon—a Core Council meeting. Tun Said wanted to know: When was it going to be? What were his plans? 'Just ask around,' he'd said. 'No one would suspect you, you look Chinese enough.'

So, the next day, Rosita and I waltzed into Central Market like two casual shoppers, but at The Annexe, we split up. 'I'll wait for you here,' she said, gesturing to the Popular Book Shop. I walked round the corner and saw a small crowd in front of me. They were largely Chinese, milling around the different booths. The table next to me had baskets of yellow badges in it with some Malay word on it. The guy behind the counter gave me a wide grin.

'Hey, Katie, right?'

He kept smiling, his skin gleaming white. 'It's Leong.' He pointed two fingers at himself like some kind of rapper. Of course, Roy's bassist. He had this bouncy, dance-y quality about him as if was talking to some kind of beat in his head. 'Want to buy a badge?' He held up a basket. 'Money goes to the Mentari Youth Club.'

'No thanks,' I said.

'How about a key chain?'

'No thanks.'

I picked up a badge, and then I put it down. 'Hey,' I said in lower voice. 'Do you know if Tony Ong is coming for this rally?' Leong narrowed his eyes at me. 'I don't know. Why?'

I shrugged. 'I just heard he might.'

'Hey, want to buy a badge?' Leong was speaking to another girl who had just come to the table. 'Talk to you later,' he whispered to me.

So I wandered around the different booths. It was a bit like a local fair. There was a booth selling potted plants, cookies, bookmarks. A booth giving out mineral water bottles and information about some opposition parties X and Y. Then there was some guy selling artwork that was actually pretty good. I contemplated getting Dessi some graffiti art with the Twin Towers on it. As I picked it up for a closer look, a girl brushed past me. 'It's starting, it's starting,' she gushed.

The crowd seemed to swell towards a particular room on the other side of the courtyard, so I followed them. Someone thrust a goodie bag into my hand, another person handed me a pamphlet. I flipped through the pages as I sat on the chair but there was nothing on Tony Ong. The only thing of interest was a write-up about the FM18 and I smiled to see Roy's band, Daytona, in the listing.

A lady came onto the stage and the audience cheered—a roomful of mostly Chinese boys and girls, perhaps in college or a bit older. There were a fair few middle-aged people but one thing was for sure, I didn't see any Malays. Applause echoed through the hall and a man's voice boomed, 'Good morning, everyone!' He was greeted by a loud cheer. I peered at the stage but a lady holding up an iPad blocked my view. 'How are you today?' the man said. 'It feels like a good day, doesn't it?'

The crowd roared at his cry, they seemed to know him and he had the kind of voice that lifted your spirits. I shifted to get a better view but found myself blocked by a particularly tall guy, so I tried the other side. And there, standing on the stage between the heads of two men, was Pa with his hair slicked to the side the way I'd seen it this morning. He smiled and waved at the crowd. He wasn't at the lawyers'. He was here, in a public hall speaking to about 500 people.

Was it really him? Pa did not speak in front of crowds, he pottered in the garden or squinted in front of his computer. He packed biscuits in a factory. 'I'm glad to see so many of you here today,' he said. 'Do you know what this means?'

I sat there for ten minutes, unable to believe that that was him. He spoke about the upcoming elections, stepping up and taking action. He spoke about the return of Tony Ong. The information came to me in pieces, like a transmission that was cutting in and out. Could he see me? Did he know I was there? I sunk deeper into my seat. I felt like I was underwater and couldn't breathe. As soon as the next break arrived, I got up and ran out of the hall.

* * *

Back at the Wira canteen, Rosita and I managed to find a table near the window. The sun sliced the table into warm, golden wedges but I still felt cold. 'You okay?' she said.

'Yeah, I'm okay.'

'How come you suddenly got a stomachache?'

'I don't know.'

I did not see Tun Said come until he was right next to the table. 'Hello,' he said. 'What's wrong?'

'She's sick,' said Rosita.

'I'm okay.' I sat up. 'Better now.'

Tun Said narrowed his eyes at me. 'How was the rally?'

'It was okay.'

'Did you see anything interesting?'

'Not really.' My heart thudded. 'Just some Chinese lady.'

'Anyone else?'

I gripped my cup. Did he know? Had it all been a test? 'My father was there,' I said. I put down my cup and met his gaze.

'Yes, your father is Paul Chen, isn't he?' He smiled faintly, his eyes, neutral.

'Did you know he was going to be there?'

'No, but I had a feeling he might be. He's been helping the Teluk Intan candidate a lot.'

I stayed silent. A heat was simmering in my chest. The pieces began to fall into place. Teluk Intan—wasn't that near Ipoh? Is that why he was always there?

'What did he talk about?' said Tun Said casually.

'I'm not sure, I left before he finished.'

'Lucky I sent Firhad then.'

'Firhad? He managed to get in?'

Firhad was as Malay as one could get. I couldn't imagine him walking in without anyone noticing. 'He didn't have to go in,' said Tun Said. 'He knows people there.'

'That's good.' I sat up straighter. 'What did he say?'

'Well, we know the Core Council meeting is on Friday. But we are not sure where it is.' Tun Said cocked his head to one side. 'Are you?'

'No,' I said. 'I have no idea. I had to leave early.'

'You didn't see Suzanna there, did you?'

'No, was she there?'

'Yes, I believe so. I think she meets with your father quite often. Did you know that?'

The memory of Suzanna and Pa talking in her house that day flew in like a big fat pie. 'Are you sure? I don't think they're that close.' I guess I could lie pretty well if I needed to. Suzanna arrived at that moment, her hijab fluttering gently under the motion of the fan. 'Tea?' she said, placing a tray onto the table.

'Assalamulaikum,' said Tun Said. 'How are you?'

'Good. And you?' She lifted up the teapot and poured out a stream of tea. 'Careful,' she said. 'It's hot.'

'That's okay.' The water must have been boiling but Tun Said picked it up like it was an apple, his hands clasped around the burning glass. 'I haven't see you around much lately,' he said. 'What have you been up to?'

'Oh, the usual. Been busy with the Hari Raya Haji event. Some of the children want to do a performance, so we've been practising some *syair* songs.'

'Nice,' said Tun Said.

Suzanna poured out another cup of tea for me. The topaz liquid streamed into the glass. 'Were you near Central Market this morning by any chance?' Tun Said continued.

'No,' she replied.

'Someone said they saw you there.'

'Really? Maimunah and I were making gift bags for the Conversion Ceremony. We are planning to make potpourri. Or do you think a candle would be better?'

Tun Said pressed his lips together. 'Either one is fine.'

After Suzanna and Tun Said left, Rosita sipped on a box of sugarcane juice. She glanced at Tun Said and his crew sitting at another table. 'They must still be discussing that missing notebook.'

'You think?'

'Yep, they have been asking everyone.'

'What is in it?'

'Some plans they have for the next few months. Apparently it's highly confidential. Tun Said has been particularly annoyed ever since he found out it was missing.' Rosita sighed. 'I'm so tired of all this. I wish they could just find out where the Core Council meeting is.'

'Why?'

'So they can end all this fighting.'

'What do you mean?'

'Tun Said wants to talk to them but they don't want to listen.'

'Doesn't he want to fight?'

'Of course not, Islam is about peace. I heard though that the Mentari people are planning something. Tony Ong is back and they're all getting a bit riled up.'

'I see.'

Tun Said leaned over to Firhad and a few other men. They kept looking across the room at Suzanna. I could tell they were not happy with her. She stood next to Maimunah, wrapping up some *kuih* in banana leaves, oblivious to all the suspicion directed at her.

Her tea filled my mouth with a profusion of flavours. To Tun Said, it was just tea. But I could tell it was a black tea with notes of goji berry and cypress. I knew what went into making a single concoction; everything was measured and considered, nothing left to chance.

I knew all these things and yet, there was so much I also didn't know about her. I thought of Pa and her in the house that day. Was she working with him? Whose side was she on? I didn't have the answers but I knew one thing. I had to stop Tun Said from finding out. As he got up from the table, I got up too. I put down my cup and walked purposefully towards him.

Chapter 36

Room

When I went to Suzanna's house later that day, no one seemed to be home. 'Hello?' I said, knocking the door. I moved the baju kurung I was carrying to my other hand; the plastic crinkled on the hanger. 'Suzanna?' I tried the doorknob and it twisted.

'Suzanna!' I said, stepping inside.

'Suzanna?' I said more softly.

Everything seemed to be covered by a thin blanket so delicate that if I spoke too loudly, it might break. There was something sweet in the air like jasmine. A teacup sat on the dining table with a teaspoon resting beside it. The rest of the table was spotless, just a floral pink tablecloth protected by clear plastic. No sign of any notebook. The sideboard was in perfect order, everything neatly put away. The only items on the counter were a stack of magazines and a spectacles case.

A small sound rustled in the kitchen. I put my bag and clothes down and made my way in. 'Suzanna?' I said, stepping onto the tiled floor. Encik Nasir was sitting on the mat, licking his paws. The Aztec patterns on the fabric surrounded him in layers of red, purple and black as if he was some kind of royalty. Everything in the kitchen seemed exactly as it should be. Eight cups sitting on the shelf. The linoleum table wiped clean. Max Benez's voice slipped slowly down the hallway, beckoning me in.

'Hello!' I said, squinting into the shadows. The cat meowed and followed me. It rubbed its tangerine body around my calf, tickling my skin with its fur. I followed the music down the corridor until I reached a sliver of light.

The door to the last room was open! This was my chance. The triangle of light on the floor reeled me in. It would have the answer to everything. Who was Suzanna—was she actually working for the Mentari people? Why was she helping them? I was almost 100 per cent sure I would find the notebook in there.

I pushed the door open half-expecting to see Suzanna there, but there was no one. Just a great big desk reigning over the room. It was the shelf behind, however, that I couldn't stop staring at. It started from one end of the wall and stretched all the way to the other. A shelf filled with hundreds and hundreds of jars.

I read the labels slowly—'Hempseed', 'Goldenrod', 'Kacip Fatimah'—all written in an elegant cursive script. I continued to inch my way from left to right until my hip bumped into something on the desk. It was Suzanna's green notebook.

My pulse raced. Was this what the fuss was all about? A grey satin ribbon stuck out at the bottom, inviting me to lift the page. I opened the book and saw Suzanna's scrawl inside, the same writing that labelled the jars, and that photograph Lily had given to me. The words flew across the pages like mathematical equations: 'Cinderwood 3, Helichrysum 10, Wintergreen 8 + Camphor 2.'

Many ingredients had been cancelled or adjusted. The '2' struck off, replaced by a '1.5'. A note written on the side in impossibly small font: 'Add Cypress?' No matter how messy and complex the page got, Suzanna's script remained neat and legible.

'What are you doing here?' Suzanna called out from the door.

'Sorry,' I said. ' I saw the door open and I thought you—'

'Give me that.'

I handed her the notebook.

'Why are you here?' she asked again.

'I said I would drop by to show you my baju kurung—for the Conversion Ceremony tomorrow,' I added. There was a flicker of recollection in Suzanna's eyes. She frowned and flicked her gaze towards the hall where the white baju kurung lay waiting on a chair. The book was still in her hand. She slipped it back into the pocket of her robe. I didn't quite understand what was in it. But I knew it wasn't what Tun Said was looking for.

Chapter 37

Blood

It was the day of the Conversion Ceremony and I was trying to tie my headscarf the way Suzanna did. How did she manage to get it to hang so evenly? I pushed a pin in above my ear but the mirror revealed the left side cinched up. As I took a step back, I heard a loud thud downstairs. Who could that be? It was Siti's day off and Tua Khor was out playing mah-jong. I quickly took the scarf off and dashed out to the stairs.

'Katie?' the voice called. 'You there?'

I ran down and saw Justin, Roy and Nasa—in that order. The three of them huddled through the front door. My heart lurched when I saw the blood on Justin's sleeve. 'Are you okay?'

'It's not me,' said Justin. 'It's him.' Roy clutched his arm and I saw the scratches above his elbow. His small eyes squinted even smaller as he peered at me.

'What happened?'

'Do you have a first-aid kit?' said Justin.

'I'll check.'

I ran to the kitchen and found one in a cupboard. When I got back to the living room, Shang had appeared. Roy was still slumped in an armchair, his head in a stiff, awkward position as if he was afraid to move it. A trickle of blood slid down his left arm. Justin took out some cottonwool and a bottle of blue liquid.

He seemed to know exactly what to do with it, as if he'd done this sort of thing before.

He rolled up Roy's sleeve and began to clean the wound. As he dabbed away the blood, he told me what happened. He and Nasa were leaving Pete's Place when they saw a bunch of people crowding around the old school building, 'you know, the one across the field?'

'We were at the Core Council meeting,' Shang added.

The words sent a chill down my gut into the pits of my stomach. Justin said he didn't know what started it, but a huge fight broke out. People were hitting each other with chairs and sticks. One guy even had a *parang*. They saw Roy and Shang near the front gate. Roy could barely stand up. The police were coming and people were running away so he and Nasa brought them to their car. Roy groaned and shifted.

'Chill, bro,' said Justin. 'Almost done.'

Clangy music pierced the air. Shang got up and spoke loudly into his phone. Just as he hung up, his phone trilled again. He started talking, pacing up and down the hall. When the calls stopped coming, he came over. 'Roy okay?' he said. 'Roy, you okay?' Roy didn't reply. But I saw him rotate his head towards Shang. Blood-stained cotton on the table. A blue ice pack on Roy's head. The reality of what had happened hit me. I imagined people wielding knives, slashing each other like some kind of *Braveheart* movie scene. 'Why did they bring weapons?' I muttered to myself.

'What?' said Nasa, sitting up. His fringe was swept upwards, slick and furious. There was steel in his eyes.

'The Mentari people,' I said. 'Why did they bring weapons?'

'They didn't bring any weapons. It was the Wira people. They have a whole arsenal of weapons in their store room. Batons, parangs, even tear gas.'

'How do you know?' I said.

'I've seen it.' He gritted his teeth. 'In that shed in Tun Said's garden.'

Nasa's words flicked a switch in my head. 'That night at Tun Said's house,' I said. 'Is that what you were doing there?' I recalled him there, always watching, always waiting; sneaking around the canteen or lurking amidst the trees. 'It's you,' I blurted, narrowing my eyes at him. 'Are you the one that has been passing information to the Mentari people?'

Nasa folded his arms. 'How about the notebook?' I said. 'Did you take the notebook?' I recalled the way Nasa had clutched his bag that night but before he could reply, Roy groaned. He shifted and muttered something to the floor. 'What?' I leaned forward. Roy winced again. He made a small sound between a sigh and a moan. The words came out in pieces: 'I don't know . . . how . . . they knew.'

'Knew what?' I asked.

'I don't know how they knew we were there,' he mumbled.

A coldness rushed through my throat. I had no choice. He was going to go after Suzanna. That day at The Annex, as I was leaving, Leong had come up to me. 'So, you support Tony Ong?' he said. I nodded. He told me about the Core Council meeting, the meeting of leaders. Everyone will be there. You can come too. 'It will be at "the school".'

I was not going to say a word to anyone. Really. But when I saw Tun Said approaching Suzanna, I knew I had to do something. He promised it was just to talk. He said there would be no fighting. Roy flailed his hands in front of his body and tried to sit up. 'What are you doing?' I said, my heart in my throat. 'Sit down.'

'I have to go to the concert,' he said.

'Are you crazy?' I said, feeling slightly dizzy. 'You can't go.'

A 'bing' sound filled the room. Shang checked his phone and said, 'Tiger's Eye is pulling out, their lead singer is hurt.'

Roy frowned.

'Rope is pulling out too,' Shang continued. 'They're all scared.'

'That's why we need to go,' declared Roy. He put down his ice pack and stood up. He took a few steps then stopped. I felt sick to the bone, as if I had plunged a knife into him and made that wound on his arm, a red spot on the plaster which was beginning to grow.

'Come on, Roy,' said Shang. 'Leong's not going either. He just messaged.'

Roy sat back on the couch and stared at the carpet. It was so quiet, I could hear the clock ticking on the wall. A bevy of buzzes rang from Shang's phone like bells chasing after each other. Justin sat across from me, his back straight on the rosewood chair. He had not said anything all this while. But this time, he cleared his throat and said, 'Katie.'

'Yeah?'

'Your father was there too.'

Chapter 38

Hospital

The moment Justin turned into the foyer, I jumped out of the car. I squinted at the signs in different languages. They blended into each other, the Malay words weaving into the English. I spotted the word 'Reception' and followed it to the front desk.

The nurse behind the counter was busy writing something. 'Is there a Paul Chen here?' I asked, between breaths.

'Huh?' she replied.

I tried to make my accent as neutral as possible. 'Is there a Paul Chen here? He's my father.' The nurse examined her clipboard. Then she switched to her computer. It seemed like she was looking at it for hours. Time crept as I watched the blue pen clipped to her pocket. The stack of post-it notes on the table. Her name tag flashing 'Hafiza'. Finally, she looked up and said, 'Room three-oh-two.'

I didn't knock. I went straight in and saw him lying motionless on the bed. I wanted to rush over and grab him but all I could do was stand there frozen. Loud sobs came out of my body and my chest heaved up and down. I had never cried like that before, not even when I thought mum had died. Guilt, remorse, grief—they all rolled into one and kept bowling me over, wave after wave, until I had no strength left to stand. When the weeping subsided, I trod slowly towards him.

There was a plaster on his cheek and his arm was in a brace. He murmured, 'Hi.' A flood of relief flowed through my body. 'I was worried about you,' he said.

'You were worried . . . about *me*?'

Pa smiled, or at least his eyes did. 'I told you to go back to Melbourne, didn't I?'

'Did you know this was going to happen?' I asked, studying his swollen eye.

He tilted his head in a way that was neither a yes or a no. Tubes connected his left arm to a packet of liquid on a pole. 'Are you okay?' I said.

'I'm okay.' He shifted his body up higher. He said he didn't remember much. There was a fight. People running around. Then everything went black. When he came to, he was in the back seat of a car. 'I'm sorry,' I cried, the words catching in my throat.

'For what?'

'It's my fault you're here. I was the one that told them where the meeting was.'

Pa shook his head sagely. 'They would have found out anyway.' A trolley clattered outside the door. It grew loud then faded away. 'I'm glad you're here,' he said. 'All through the car ride, I was thinking about what you said. I should have told you the truth earlier.'

I clicked my tongue. 'It's okay. I was just angry.'

'I always wanted to tell you but I kept putting it off. I thought maybe when she's ten, maybe when she's thirteen, then after a while, it seemed too late.'

The liquid on the pole gurgled and I felt a strange sense of reality. 'So it was all a lie?' I said wistfully. 'She didn't have pneumonia, she just didn't want to come back?'

'Actually,' Pa said, his voice stronger. 'She was unwell. She didn't want me to tell you this but . . . she's got depression.'

'I know. That's why she stopped her music.'

Pa narrowed his eyes. 'Well, it's a bit more than that. Your mother always had a problem with . . . being happy. She was like that when I first met her. She was happy most of the time but she had these . . . dark moments, as she called them. Nothing could get her out except writing music. She would write the most brilliant songs then and when she finished them, she would be all good again. That was just her.'

Pa smiled as he said this and I could see the memories in his eyes. 'But as time went by, the dark moments became more frequent and the songs could no longer help. In fact, it made her even more upset when she couldn't finish them. It was like a puzzle she couldn't solve and it just drove her deeper into the darkness.'

Pa said it got worse when she came to Melbourne. He thought starting afresh in a new place would make it better but one day, he came home and found her sitting in a corner in the kitchen. 'She had just come back from grocery shopping and you had half a jar of peanut butter on your face.'

The puppy dog bowl flashed before me. 'I remember that day.'

'You do?'

'Yes, she bought oranges too.'

'She did? I don't know, but that was the first time it happened. Another time, she came back in tears because some white woman at the supermarket yelled at her to go back to her own country.'

'I mean these things would bother anyone, but I think it bothered her more than others. Migrating is like being a plant that is pulled from its roots. Usually you can regrow, you might look like you're dying for a while but after some time, you get used to the soil and you grow high and strong and thrive in the new land.' Pa gripped his blanket. 'She didn't.'

He continued, 'She found it hard that she had to do a lot of things on her own. She couldn't just pop over to the neighbours'

with you. We didn't have an aunt coming over with chicken curry.
We did everything ourselves.'

I'd never heard Pa speak to me so much before. It felt like
we were both grown-ups. 'I think what she struggled with most
was being away,' he said. 'She missed the things around her—the
people, the food, the noises . . .'

'The buzz,' I interjected.

'Sorry?'

'She missed the buzz.'

'Yes, I suppose you could call it that. Actually, that's a good
description! When she went back to Malaysia to see her father, she
didn't want to come back. She kept making excuses. She said she
needed to sort out his estate stuff. She had to help her aunt. After
some time, the thought of going back filled her with so much
dread, she would have panic attacks.'

Pa fingered the identification band on his list. 'Remember that
weekend I had to go to Malaysia and Diana took care of you?'

I shook my head.

'I went back to see her then, to bring her home, but she just
couldn't do it. She . . . .' Pa's voice trailed off. 'She didn't want to
live anymore.'

Was it that bad? Had she tried to end her life? I pictured
hanging, pills, cutting her wrists. No, I couldn't even imagine it.
Pa continued talking. 'It's an illness,' he said. 'She didn't want me
to tell you about it. She just wanted you to carry on with the good
memories.' It was so quiet, I could hear the buzz of electricity
from the lights above us. A machine hummed near the wall.

'So, it wasn't because of me?' I surmised.

'Of course not, did you think that all this while?'

* * *

I thought I was the one who made her cry. She would say,
'stop stressing me out, Katie. I'm tired, I'm just so tired. You're

making me so tired.' At playgroup, I would draw her pictures or make her things with playdough, but nothing could make her happy. I remember giving her something I'd made and she said, 'That's nice, Katie' but her eyes were empty. I felt like she was somewhere else, like she wanted to be anywhere else but stuck with me.

Pa's eyes were closed and I thought he had fallen asleep but then he opened them again. 'I knew I should have told you earlier,' he said. 'But things were a bit messy for me, too. Diana kept telling me I wasn't over it and I had to move on but I didn't realize what she meant. I just concentrated on doing what I had to do each day and after a while, everything seemed too far away.'

Suddenly, I had an epiphany: Pa and I, waiting to see Diana in the waiting room. He going in first and then me. Diana wasn't just *my* psychologist. She was his too. Pieces of the past began to unravel. Pa making me noodles and red bean buns, sizzling roast pork so exquisite, I could taste it in my mouth right then—as he worked away in silence, not saying a word but always making sure I was there close to him. I remembered us walking on the beach in winter, tipping over stones to look for starfish and seaweed. I remembered him staring out at the ocean with that faraway look in his eyes I now knew was sadness.

'Do you still love her?' I asked.

'Of course,' he said. 'I will always love her.' A heavy weight lodged in my chest. 'What about Diana?' I asked softly.

Pa folded the soft cotton of the blanket. 'With your mum, it was a different kind of love,' he explained. 'You know how sometimes the way you remember something isn't actually real? It starts off as a memory then it grows into something else, and the only way you can realize it for what it is, is when it's standing in front of you.' Pa sat up and leaned closer, 'When I saw her again that day in the village, that day you saw us, that's how I felt.'

'I love your mum,' Pa said. 'But I know I can't be with her. I don't know why it took me so long to realize this.' Pa let out a sigh. And when he did, his whole body seemed to relax. There was even a slight smile on his face. 'I'm not making sense, am I?'

'You are, you are,' I said. 'But maybe you should tell her that.'

'Who?'

I handed my phone to Pa, Diana's message still open on my screen.

* * *

As Pa drifted in and out of sleep, I examined the picture on the wall, a photograph of river stones stacked up in a way that was supposed to be calming. I'd seen similar pictures at various psychology clinics in Melbourne. I smiled at the thought that there was this one person supplying clinics and hospitals around the world.

'You're still here.' Pa's eyes were open again and he looked slightly more alert. His hair was dishevelled, his hospital gown crumpled, but there was a presence to him I had never noticed before.

'So,' I said. 'You're some sort of opposition leader?'

'I just have a blog.' He shrugged.

'Why didn't you ever tell me about it?'

'I didn't think you would understand. Even Diana didn't.' He let out a sigh. 'I just continued writing like how I did at the paper and people seemed to like it. They wanted real information, they wanted the truth.'

'The truth.' I stifled a smile, thinking about the truth that had been hidden from me all these years.

'Are you angry?' he said.

'About what?'

'That I didn't tell you about the blog.'

I shrugged. 'No, it's okay.'

Pa tried to scratch his head but when he realized there was a bandage around his palm, he lowered his hand. 'Writing helped me focus on things,' he said almost to himself. 'It helped me get through the day.'

'Was it hard to get through?'

Pa pondered the weave of the blanket. 'It was hard to work,' he concluded. 'I didn't feel like working in journalism again, or in an office, or anywhere corporate.'

I looked at Pa in mock innocence. 'What's wrong with the biscuit factory?'

Pa studied my expression, trying to figure out if I was joking. 'I guess it's not a real job.'

'Isn't it?' I smiled. I was just glad Pa was alive and moving, and not in pain.

* * *

We settled into a comfortable silence after a while. Pa stared at the wall, a sliver of light zigzagging across the mounds of his blanket. 'I'm so sick of this room,' he said with a sigh. 'Everything's so stuffy.'

'Can you walk?' I said. 'Do you want me to take you outside?'

The nurse gave me a wheelchair to push him around in. We did a circuit of Ward B, passing room after room, the nurse's reception, an X-Ray room and back to Pa's room again. 'Is there anywhere else to go?' Pa said.

I squinted around and saw a sign that said 'Courtyard' and wheeled Pa in that direction. A tuft of black hair stuck out of his bandaged head as the wheels of the wheelchair rolled down the corridor. We came up to a large window which opened into a courtyard of trees. And that's where we parked. Pa in his wheelchair and me on the sofa. The both of us soaking up this sanctuary amidst the cold, medical tools.

Golden sun melted all over Pa but I could still see the dent on his brow. He had his hands on his lap, one on top of the other, and I could see how his skin had aged. The sound of thunder rumbled across the sky and rain began to fall on the leaves. Pa kept staring out at the plants and for a moment, I thought of taking out a book to read. In the end, I sat there and studied the plants with him, watching the leaves flicker under the touch of rain.

'Look,' I said, pointing at a fir-like tree.

'What?'

'That tall tree at the back.'

I showed Pa the light that came out of the tree, the shimmer of each dewdrop gripping to a branch. 'I love it when that happens,' I said, beaming. Pa turned to me with a smile then he went back to looking at the rain.

* * *

After the shower subsided, Pa caught my gaze. 'There is one more thing I haven't told you,' he said.

I sat up.

'Have you heard of Alzheimer's?' he said.

'Yes, it's when you forget things, right?'

He nodded. 'Your mother just found out she has it.'

A bitter taste developed in my mouth. 'Isn't she a bit young for that?'

'It's early-onset Alzheimer's. Her dad had it too.' Pa paused. ''That's how he died.'

'I didn't know you could die from Alzheimer's. I thought it just made you forget things.'

'It's a disease of the brain so you end up forgetting things but in the end, you can also forget how to eat or drink or move.'

I felt a hard pellet in my chest. 'Is she going to die?'

'I don't know. There is no cure, but she does seem more depressed lately.'

The moment Pa said that, something clicked in my head. I recalled Suzanna's notebook and the words scribbled on numerous pages. 'Alzheimer's. Early onset Alzheimer's.' Amidst all the formulas and calculations, those same words kept repeating themselves. The jars on the wall. The notes, jotted down over months and years, an entire life's work dedicated to finding an answer. She was trying to cure herself.

I saw Pa's eyelids drooping and I pushed him back to his room. The nurse tucked him back into bed and soon, he fell asleep. I sat on the worn chair, listening to the electricity sizzling behind the walls. I thought of Suzanna walking around, feeling lost, angry with herself, angry with the world, and I knew she needed me now more than ever.

Chapter 39

Will You Play?

When I walked out into the foyer, I saw Justin waiting for me on a black leather couch. But as I got closer, I saw that Roy was there too, as were Nasa and Shang, everyone sitting around as if it was someone's living room. 'You went to see a doctor?' I asked Roy, eyeing the plaster on his temple.

'Yup.' He waved one of his crutches in the air. 'How's your dad?'

'He's okay.' I glanced at the three boys sitting around the table. 'You still waiting for the doctor?'

'No, actually, we were waiting for you.' Roy shifted his crutch and glanced at Shang. 'I heard you're pretty good on the guitar,' Shang said.

I frowned, the three of them were staring at me. Shang said a lot of bands had pulled out of the FM18. But they were planning to go ahead. Leong couldn't play because he was a bit shaken up. Shang scratched the back of his ear. 'Can you play with us?'

'Oh no.' I shook my head. 'I'm not that good—'

'She's good,' blurted Nasa. 'I've heard her play. I think she can pretty much play anything by ear.'

'Is that true?' Roy said. 'You've been going for our practice sessions. Can you play "Everlong"?'

'I think I can . . . but—'

'That's awesome,' said Roy, jerking up. 'Will you do it, Katie? That would be so great.'

I shook my head. 'I can't.'

'Why?'

A lady walked past outside. She had a bluish-grey headscarf just like Suzanna's.

'I have something else on.'

'Katie, this is a one-off event,' said Shang. 'It's not going to happen again.'

'I know. But I can't. I have something else on at the same time.'

Shang narrowed his eyes at me; his gold necklace, twinkling. 'What is it?'

'She's going for the Wira event,' said Nasa in his calm, deep voice.

Roy snapped his head towards me. 'The conversion ceremony?' he said. 'Is that true?'

I scanned the faces of each one of them—Nasa, Shang, Roy. 'How are you going to play anyway?' I asked Roy, 'You can't even walk properly.'

Roy's leg was stretched out in front of him in a moon boot. 'I'm not playing,' he replied. 'Justin is covering for me.'

All this while, I hadn't really noticed Justin sitting quietly on a corner sofa. 'You're playing?' I said, watching him fiddle with a square piece of paper.

'Yep.' He looked up and blinked.

'I thought you didn't want to get involved.'

'I thought you said I was not involved enough.'

The aircon blasted down on us. I could smell the scent of mi goreng from the nearby cafeteria, the oily aroma making my stomach churn. 'I'm sorry,' I said, turning back to Roy. 'I can't. I have to be at the Wira event.'

Roy rolled his eyes and leaned over to Nasa. Justin turned to me. 'Why do you need to go there?' he asked in a low, quiet voice.

I felt a lump form in my throat. Justin tilted his head. 'Are you converting?'

Roy and the others stopped talking and turned to look at me. 'Are you?' I turned away to face the sunlight streaming through the glass doors. Justin kept his gaze one me.

'You've found your mum,' he said. 'You hang out with her, why do you need to convert?'

I gripped my bag, my palms wet. 'I want to,' I said, averting his gaze.

'Do you?'

'Yes.' I said, meeting his eyes, but when I did, my hands felt even colder.

Roy and Shang burst into an argument with Nasa interjecting from time to time. 'I told you we couldn't trust her,' said Shang.

'I don't know why she is doing this.'

'It doesn't make sense.

Finally, Roy stepped back and turned to me. 'You really can't play?' I felt my heart wringing in my chest like I was being torn both ways. I saw the earnest expression on Roy's face and really wanted to help but then I remembered Suzanna, the way she stood at the junction, crying, slowly slipping away. 'Sorry,' I said, hitching up my bag. 'I need to go.'

Chapter 40

Conversion Day

'Come on,' said Rosita. 'This way.' We hitched up the skirts of our white baju kurungs and made our way towards the west gate of Dataran Merdeka. On the east side, a queue was already forming to get into the FM18 event.

When I stepped into the stadium, I saw the Wira marquees all lined up. Green flags flew high and people milled around in long, white robes. Rosita slid into one of the tents and unzipped her bag. She took out a brush and began brushing her hair. Faint sounds of rock music drifted in. 'I thought the FM18 would be cancelled,' Rosita commented. 'Are there many people out there?'

I stepped up onto a box and peeped over the barrier. 'Yep,' I said. There must have been at least a thousand people out there. 'There are so many Malays,' I murmured. I thought the event would have more Chinese if it was anything like the Central Market rally. A dark-skinned boy was jumping up and down. For some reason, he was wearing a tie and it flew up and down over his black T-shirt. 'Are they all here for the music?'

Rosita stood on tiptoe beside me. 'Maybe not,' she replied. A group of Malay youth were raising their fists in the air. Another group was weaving its way through the crowd. A knot tightened in my gut. Was this some kind of secret attack? I recalled what Nasa has said about the weapons he'd seen in the shed, like they were preparing for something big. Maybe the fight in the school was not the main event, maybe this was the real battle.

I watched these groups of Malay youth—mostly boys— start to infiltrate the crowd. Did Roy know? I messaged him: Are you okay?

No reply came. I watched two Malay boys at the side whisper to each other, scanning the area like they were planning something. I checked my phone again and Roy had still not messaged.

'Come on,' said Rosita. 'Let's get ready.'

We went back inside and Rosita held out a gold flower to me. 'Can you help?'

'Sure.'

I picked up a bobby pin and pinned the flower to her hair. I placed each pin carefully along the stem of the flower. When I finished, she started doing the same for me. Each pin she placed pulled my hair in tighter and tighter. I felt like staying and running away at the same time.

'Hey, Rosita.'

'Yeah?' She stirred through the box of pins. The lace on her blouse gleamed like a bride's.

'Do you have enough clips?' I said in a slightly shaky voice.

'Yeah.' She picked out a black bobby pin. She inserted the pin softly but firmly and grinned.

'What?' I said. Her eyeliner made her look like some kind of princess.

'I'm so glad you're here.' She took my hand and squeezed it. 'Can you believe it? We're actually doing this!'

'Yeah.' I smiled back weakly.

Just as I finished with my hair, Suzanna stepped into the tent. 'Katie,' she exclaimed. 'You look lovely!' She foraged through her handbag and said, 'I have something for you.' The box was made of grey velvet like rabbit's fur. I prised it open and saw the brooch inside. It was a silver orchid on a bed of white satin. 'My mother gave it to me at my conversion ceremony. I thought you might like it.'

'Are you sure? Is it a religious thing?

'No, no, not at all; it's more like a family thing.'

A *family* thing. The word sent a thrill through me. I thought of family dinners, family holidays, people sitting around the dinner table. The brooch looked exactly like a real flower. If you looked closely enough, you could even see tiny specks glittering between the grooves.

'Are those diamonds?' I whispered.

'No,' said Suzanna. 'It's selenite.'

Selenite was a special crystal that gave courage and clarity. Suzanna's mother believed in things like that. Crystals, stones, lucky charms. I imagined her as some sort of witch in a shimmery silver robe.

Suzanna took out the brooch and pinned it to my collar. If there was a doorway to exit what I was about to do, it had suddenly grown smaller. The brooch shone under my chin. Maybe it did have a power. I turned to face the mirror and I saw a girl in a white baju kurung with just the slightest frown on her face.

Chapter 41

Waiting

There was really nothing left for me to do. My hair was tied. I had some makeup on. I reached for my selendang and slipped it over my head. The scarf draped softly across my shoulders and yet I found it hard to breathe.

I stepped outside. There were people drifting around in groups of three or four, other tents on the other side of the field. Green flags waved wildly in the wind as the Nashid girls swished past, leaving a trail of song and music in their wake. It felt like a marketplace and I needed to find some space to breathe. I wove through the crowd as if I knew exactly where I was going. When I passed Maimunah, she tried to catch my eye but I pretended not to see her. I bent down respectfully with my arm leading the way as Rosita had taught me, and hurried past.

I kept walking until I reached the bleachers. I climbed up to the top and gazed out at the sky. The clouds were rimmed in gold like on a picture-perfect postcard, the Twin Towers rising in the distance. I scanned through my phone and Googled Pa's name: 'Paul Chen'.

A series of articles appeared. They were all about Malaysia—the Yellow Spring, the rise of a new Malaysia, a call for clean elections—each with heaps of likes and comments. But one particular piece caught my eye: 'Stories for my daughter'.

It appeared to be a letter of sorts.

'I wish I could tell you what life was like before. I wish I could tell you stories about my childhood but that's all they will ever be. Stories. The country I knew before doesn't exist anymore.'

I scrolled down.

'There are so many things I love about this country, and I didn't want to leave. But I'm not sure if I can really change anything anymore. I just realized it's not the same country I grew up in and I'm not sure it can ever be.'

This seemed to be his most recent article and I could feel the dejection in his words. I scrolled down further and saw a picture of Pa and another man, standing side by side. The caption said: 'Paul Chen and Tony Ong speak at a Mentari rally in Teluk Intan'. I studied the picture again. I couldn't stop staring at it. I almost didn't recognize Pa. I'd never seen his eyes so bright and determined before. I'd never seen him look so alive.

The strains of music drifted over from the other side of the field. I could see the FM18 stage in the distance marked by two yellow banners. It felt like a battlefield. Green over here, yellow over there. My bun felt tight and I began pulling the pins out of my hair. I shook it loose and just as I did, Rosita came up. 'What are you doing?'

'I can't go through with this,' I said, sweeping the clips into my hand.

'Why?'

'I just can't.' I said, clenching my fists.

Rosita watched me fold up my scarf and tuck it underneath my arm. 'I didn't think you would,' she said in a quiet voice.

'Really?'

'I can tell you don't really believe in it. During the last few classes, you kept staring out the window.'

I smiled and looked down at my hands. 'You're right. It's been bothering me for a while.'

'How about me?' Rosita said. 'You're not going to stop me?'

'No. Why?'

Rosita narrowed her eyes at me and tilted her head.

'It's not about the religion,' I blurted. 'I love the teachings, I love the philosophy. It's me. There is something I need to do first.'

Chapter 42

Concert

The bands hadn't come on yet but people were already dancing to the music playing. I stopped to check my phone. Still no word from Roy. The crowd still looked largely Malay. I spotted a group of them whispering to each other near the speakers. They wore backpacks and strange long jackets. Were they hiding something underneath?

A boy spilled out of a mosh pit and landed in front of me. He glanced up, laughed, and jumped back in. The drums began to beat more loudly, the guitars built up to a frenzy. Amidst this chaos, I spotted Roy standing on a platform backstage. I climbed up the steps and made my way towards him. A guy in an Afro squeezed past, another guy sat on a box, tapping his fingers.

In the corner, I saw Justin standing, peering out at the crowd with his arms folded. I recognized his long curls straight away, the firmness of his gaze. Then I noticed the shiny sticker on his guitar case—it was the silver star, unmistakably handmade with its uneven globs of glitter. I couldn't believe he'd kept it. A warm feeling grew inside me but it quickly disappeared when I spotted Roy.

I hurried over and called out to him. Everything seemed louder up there. The guitar riffs. The drums vibrating under my feet. When Roy saw me, his expression changed. 'What are you doing here?'

'You can't go on,' I said, above the sounds of the music.

'Why?'

'I think Tun Said is up to something. Maybe something like what they did at the Core Council meeting—'

'Did they send you over to stop us?' Roy said, glaring.

'What are you talking about?'

'Shouldn't you be at your event? It should be starting soon.' Industrial fans blew over our heads, scattering my hair all over the place.

'I don't think I belong there,' I said not sure if Roy could hear me. I could barely hear him. Then through the gushing and blaring sounds, I heard his reply. 'Do you belong here?'

* * *

The piped music stopped and the lights dimmed. The first band strode onto the stage, four shadows taking their place under the spotlight. As soon as they started playing, the audience jeered. 'Boo! Boo!' The four guys kept playing. The crowd kept booing. I watched Roy and the others. Every now and then, the lights flashed, illuminating different expressions: Roy frowning. Nasa pursing his lips. Justin studying the crowd.

The lead singer dipped the microphone on a final note and something flew into the air. It landed on his white jumpsuit and a small orange stain appeared. Something else came flying in and this time, it hit the amp. There was a high-pitched squeal then everything fell silent.

The lights dimmed and the emcee came on. 'That was Grasshopper with their number one hit single, "Goodbye Girl".' He mopped his brow and gave an awkward chuckle. 'Next up

is a band that just won an Asian ARIA award. Welcome . . .
Broken Hill!'

The emcee motioned to the band backstage. His grin seemed
to be plastered on someone who had been frozen. He pressed on
his earpiece. 'Sorry, we seem to be having a technical problem. We
will take a five-minute break.'

The crowd grumbled like dark clouds gathering. Someone
brightened the lights on the stage. It looked like the remnants of
an afterparty—lights too bright, litter all over the floor. Roy went
over to the emcee and whispered something in his ear.

Nasa, Justin and Shang began picking up their instruments.

'What are you doing?' I cried. 'Can't you see it's a set-up?
There are so many Malays out there.'

For some reason, Nasa glanced at Justin. Shang and Roy did
the same.

'Roy, stop them,' I said. 'You need to. I'm not lying—'

'And next we have . . . Daytona!' announced the emcee, with
the biggest frozen grin.

Chapter 43

On Stage

The moment they walked onto the stage, a cold ball grew inside me. I watched the three of them go on like I was watching a TV show without the remote. Nasa took his spot on the drums. Justin fiddled silently on his guitar. Shang stepped into the spotlight. His fringe was stylishly fluffed up, every strand perfectly in place. Wearing a military shirt with brass buttons, he looked like he was about to go to war. Justin started plucking a couple of strings on his guitar. I knew the song—it was a Foo Fighters cover.

The crowd rumbled. They sounded like a pack of snarling dogs. The music was drowned by the noise—it was too loud. Shang stopped singing. Justin put down his guitar. Nasa stopped playing too. He was waving at me, making strange contortions with his mouth.

'What?' I said.

'They. Want. Ratu!' Nasa said.

'What?'

'Can't you hear?'

It was as if someone had removed a glass dome from the crowd and their words jumped out from beneath. 'Ratu! Ratu!' they cried. How was this possible? How did they even know the song? Justin gestured at me, his curly hair framed in the floodlights. 'Come on,' he said. My mouth went dry. My head pounded.

It was like primary school all over again. 'Don't worry, you can do it,' my teacher would say. But I couldn't. I always couldn't. Diana said I overthought things. A fear of consequences. But I knew I was right. Everything had consequences. If I wasn't so difficult, mum wouldn't have been so tired. If I didn't give her that cough, she wouldn't have gotten sick.

'Go on, Katie,' said Roy, handing me a guitar. I gripped the guitar but my feet wouldn't move. And then it hit me. My mum wasn't dead. She was there somewhere beyond those green flags. Somewhere along the lines, the equations didn't add up. She was here and alive, and she wasn't upset because of me. *'Of course, it wasn't you. Did you think that all this while?'*

'Katie, come on.' This time the voice came from a shape above me. Justin's familiar face appeared. I knew it was him just by the outline of his shadow, from the way he tilted his head with concern. 'Come on, Katie. You're great. I know you can do it.'

I remembered the way his eyes had shone in The Shed that day, how impressed he had been. It's magical, the confidence of someone else. It can lend you a buoyancy that raises you up into places you'd never reached before. I took a deep breath and stepped into the light.

When I reached the start of the stage where the floor changed from black to polished wood, I stopped. It was as if a cavern lay between me and everyone else. My legs froze up, my heart pounded, but this time, it was different. I could feel it moving away as I willed myself to push ahead. The crowd descended into a hush to see this girl in a white baju kurung appear. This girl with wild, wavy hair, dragging her guitar onto the stage.

Chapter 44

The Real Hero

The moment I finished that last note, I knew it was good. The roar of the crowd dissipated into a sweet silence as I took in my surroundings. Everything was in slow motion: the guy cheering in the front row with his mouth wide open, the girl screaming as if she was being bowled over by a wave. A hat being thrown up high then landing on the grass with a thud. All the sound suddenly came back again—banging, cheering, talking—all at the same time.

We shuffled backstage and Nasa came over and hugged us. He showed us the 20,000 Likes the video of Justin and I had got on YouTube. 'I knew it was getting hits,' he said. 'I just didn't know by whom.'

'How did they know we were here?' I asked.

'They recognized Justin. You should have seen Tun Said's face when he came on.'

'Why?'

Nasa frowned. 'Don't you know who he is?'

Justin was down below. People were swarming all around him. Young boys and girls, Malays and Chinese, they cheered him on and patted him on the back. He smiled quietly and wove his way through the crowd.

'Tun Said is his father.' Nasa's words hit me the same time as the epiphany. The world started to spin as everything Justin told me before began to take on a slightly different meaning.

'I'm accompanying my dad to the mosque.'

'They're family friends.'

'I'm not with Wira, I hate politics.'

The impact of what he had done dawned upon me. What kind of message would that be—the Wira leader's son on stage at the FM18? I raced down the steps and scanned the crowd. Another thought hit me. 'Don't you know who your dad is?' he had said at the teh tarik stall. Had Justin already known then who Pa was? Is that why he hesitated? I combed through the crowd for Justin's face. It flashed between the shoulders of two boys. 'Justin!' I said waving to him. He disappeared. 'Justin!' I saw him emerge between a group of girls before disappearing again. As another group parted, I noticed the back of his navy blue T-shirt. 'Hey,' I said, tapping him on the shoulder.

He turned around. 'Hey,' the guy said. A guy without Justin's face. His mouth turned up into a leer as he reached out for me. I fell backwards, toppling onto the backs of people. A few minutes later, I found myself in an open space away from everyone else. And then I saw him, the shadow of him, on the other side of the field. He slipped into a small white building—the cafeteria. As I made my way there, I pieced together what I would say. I would tell him how proud I was of what he had done. I would tell him I didn't care who his father was or who mine was. I could only think about the incredible energy I felt when I was with him. He must feel it too.

I gripped the metal handles and pulled the doors open. People made their way around me as if I was a rock in the middle of a stream. Dozens of long tables filled up the cafeteria. Each table had little daisies in a small glass jar. It didn't take me long to spot Justin. He was sitting at a table on the left, hunched over a writing pad.

I was about to take another step closer when she swept in with a tray in hand. Tina, with her dark silky hair and black silky shirt; an apparition of slickness and style. I spun around and strode outside as fast as I could.

* * *

'Katie!' the voice said. 'Katie!' I turned around and saw Justin running up to me. 'Were you looking for me?'

'Uhm, no?'

'You looked like you were.' He smiled. 'Either that or you have a really bad sense of direction.'

'You looked busy.'

'I am a bit busy but I don't mind—'

'No, it's okay, Tina must be waiting for you.' I cleared my throat.

Justin looked at me with a funny smile. 'She is . . . we've got a project together.'

I continued to stare at him with a frown.

'We're doing the same course,' he added. 'I switched to Digital Design.' He told me they were working on some assignment together and the deadline was tomorrow. As his dimples flashed, light began to fall on the situation. It made me feel lighter, like I'd won a prize, and it was lifting me up off the ground.

'What happened to engineering?' I said.

'I changed my mind,' said Justin, smiling with a shrug.

We sat on a bench and went on talking. If you ask me now what we talked about, I can't say precisely what—School, dreams, food, frivolous things I can't recall. But what I remembered was laughing at the tiniest joke, at the silliest comment, and it was like once I started, I couldn't stop. I remembered a couple peering at us from another bench, and that made us burst out laughing all over again.

'Can I have one?' said Justin.

'What?'

He pointed to the bottle in my hand.

'Sure,' I said, popping him a tablet. We sat there sucking on Vitamin C pellets as the wind blew through distant trees beyond the city. When the sun slanted to touch our feet, Justin said he had to go back to the cafeteria but after he left, it still felt warm and sunny on a spot right beneath my chest.

Chapter 45

Airport

Three weeks. A lot can happen in three weeks. You can spend three weeks at a beach resort. You can learn how to surf. You can sightsee a dozen cities. Or—your whole life could change.

I went to see Suzanna one last time to return the brooch, but she said to keep it.

'It's yours,' she said, pushing my hand back to me gently. 'It's for family.' Before I left, she commented on my headscarf. 'You can never get it right, can you?' and proceeded to adjust the selendang over my head. Down, over, twist and back. 'There,' she said, beaming. That was my last image of her.

At the airport, I saw Roy, Maggie, Shang, Nasa and Leong striding into the departure area. They'd all come to see me off. 'Did you guys come together?' I said laughing. Roy and Shang eyed each other sheepishly. 'No,' said Roy. 'He followed me. Get out of here!' he said with a smile.

'Okay, you pay for the roti later,' said Shang.

'Ohh . . . you going for roti?' I gushed.

'Yeah, we're going to Newtown,' said Roy.

'I want to go too!' I said, making a face. It was so nice to see Roy and friends together with Nasa and Justin—I'd never thought it could happen.

Oh yes, Justin was there too. He stood in a corner with his hands in his pockets, peeking slyly from behind his curls. We exchanged glances from time to time, as everyone took selfies and wefies and group shots, like we were at the prom.

'Katie,' called out Leong, waving a paper bag in the air. 'I brought your favourite—durian!' He handed me the bag.

'Oh no,' I grimaced with a laugh. I opened the box and observed the T-shirt inside, the print of a cartoon durian peeking out from the folds.

'Do you like it?' Leong said. 'It's scratch and sniff!'

'Is it?' I said, holding the shirt up to my nose.

'No,' said Leong, laughing. 'But that would be a good idea, wouldn't it?'

'Thanks guys,' I said, pushing my guitar case aside.

As we stood talking, a group of tourists streamed through the Arrivals gates, pale and lost, shirking at the heat. Is that how I looked when I first arrived?

'Message on the group chat, okay?' called out Maggie. 'We'll come and visit one day.'

'Okay,' I replied, a sinking feeling in my chest.

I gave each of them a hug and when I came to Justin, I held on a few seconds longer. The scent of soap, a whiff of cigarettes. 'You been smoking?' I whispered.

'That's Leong,' he smirked. 'I was in his car.' I laughed, not sure whether or not to believe him. I did not want to let go of his hand, already so familiar, like an extension of my own.

'Come on, guys,' said Roy, clapping his hands together. 'Time to go! Katie, your dad is waiting.' And so he was. It was like ripping a band-aid off and putting water on the wound. I squeezed Justin's hand for the last time and turned towards Pa, who was standing with our bags at the Departure entrance.

* * *

When we reached our gate, Pa set up his laptop in a corner, plugging it into a power point. I chose a seat nearer to the window. A Malaysian Airlines jumbo jet was tracking across the runway. A Qantas plane languished on my right as various workers attended to her wheels and cogs and open stairways.

When I turned back to the departure lounge, I noticed an old lady smiling at me. She sat a few seats away, her hands primly clutching a little bag. Everything about her seemed tight and curled up, from her silvery perm to the way she tucked her feet under the chair.

She smiled at me sweetly and displayed a set of small, white teeth. I crossed my sneakers in front of me and straightened out the skirt of my baju kurung. The lady smiled. Finally, she leaned forward and spoke to me in a small squeaky voice.

'Are you Malay?'

'Half,' I said with a smile. 'My dad's Chinese.'

'Ahhh,' she said, nodding as if a great puzzle had been solved. 'You speak Chinese?'

'No, just English.'

The moment I said this, a feeling of lightness came over me. There was no flush, no discomfort. My voice rang clearly in the room. 'I'm from Melbourne,' I explained.

'Oh, that's nice!' The woman's eyes shone. 'My son lives there. I'm going to visit him.' She started telling me about her son in Geelong and how he was married to an Australian girl. She took out her phone and showed me pictures of them and their baby. I smiled and nodded, taking in each photo. The Botanical Gardens. Fed Square. Banksia branches winding through the trees like the ones I used to run under at the beach. When she came to the last photo, the yearning in my gut grew so large, I could smell the gum trees in the picture.

The lady went back to her seat and I felt a buzz in my bag.

Suzanna : Did you get to the airport okay?
Me   : Yes.
Suzanna : You know you can come back anytime you like, right?
Me   : Yes, I know.

I touched the orchid brooch at my throat. Sunlight fell on the silver and I imagined the petals lighting up, glowing with the hopes and dreams of my mother, her mother, and all the women who had come before me.

Suzanna : Have a good flight.
Me   : Thanks. Take care.

I sent those three words to Suzanna with as much love as one could possibly send over the internet. I'm not sure how she would be three months from now or three years from now, but I wished the best for her.

Part IV

Home

Chapter 46

Blue skies

The sky in Australia is much bigger and bluer than Malaysia. I never realized it until I came back. That was what I was thinking as I looked out of my bedroom window, at the big gum tree outside and the expansive realm of blue above. It's like taking a huge breath of air and filling up your lungs until they can't be filled anymore.

I could smell every single scent in the world and I loved it. The grass. The eucalyptus leaves. The bark of the tree in its various shades of grey and silver and silvery green. They tasted like the tea Suzanna made, each shade a different flavour, a different pinch of herb.

It had been three weeks since I left Malaysia, though it felt like much longer. The day I had been waiting for was finally here. I quickly washed up and brushed my hair. I adjusted my toner, moisturizer and lip balm on the dresser, chucked my hairbrush into the toilet case and practically ran down the stairs.

'Morning,' chirped Diana.

'Morning,' I called back.

Pa grunted.

'Do you want some breakfast?' said Diana, craning her neck as I grabbed my coat. 'Where you off to?'

'I'm meeting Dessi outside.'

'Do you want some tea?' She held up the kettle.

'No thanks!' I said. 'I'll leave you two love birds alone.'

Diana turned to Pa. 'Did she just call us "love birds"?'

Pa looked up from his iPad. Before he could reply, I chuckled and walked out the door. 'Hiya!' I said to Dessi.

'Hey,' she replied and jumped up onto the side wall. The spring morning was turning into one of those summer days where everything was bathed in a golden light. I climbed up the wall and sat next to Dessi, swinging my bare legs over the bricks. I glanced down at my hands and played with the leather band around my wrist.

'Nice dress,' she said.

'Thanks.'

I smoothed out the chiffon skirt, admiring the tiny flowers on it. The banana tree swayed in front of us, a large comb beginning to turn yellow. 'So, you sure you're not mad?' said Dessi for the fourth time that week.

'Yeah,' I said.

I smiled. I still had trouble imagining her and John Ichuda together. He in his tennis whites, she in her Doc Martens. To her credit, she had cut her hair in a really chic long bob, the purple lock now a streak of white.

'So, RMIT, huh?' said Dessi, tapping her heels against the wall. 'What made him decide on that?'

I smiled at Dessi. 'It's got a good Digital Design course.'

'Yeah,' she said with a smirk. She glanced at her giant Casio watch. 'What time is he coming?'

'Should be here anytime now.' As if on cue, a silver taxi stopped in front of the bus stop. I smiled, hopping off the wall. I patted down my skirt and flicked out my hair.

The boy stepped out of the car, lugging a suitcase and a duffel bag. He waved at the driver and the car sped off. The world shone as I walked slowly to meet him. The white picket fence gleamed with a fresh coat of paint, the banana tree blushed with a hint of a bow. The boy was a tall shape, a stranger on the sidewalk. He seemed like a glitch from a different time-zone. He peered around, his hair tumbling all over the place as if it too was unsure where to go. When I reached him, his eyes lit up and his mouth curled into a smile.

'Hi,' I said. 'Welcome to Melbourne.'

The End

Acknowledgements

Thank you to everyone who supported the journey of this manuscript: The Deborah Cass Prize Award, Kathryn Heyman, the Publishable programme by the Queensland Writers Centre and Amberdawn Manaois.